SUMMER
OF BRAVE

AMY NOELLE PARKS

Albert Whitman & Company
Chicago, Illinois

Library of Congress Cataloging-in-Publication data
is on file with the publisher.

Text copyright © 2021 by Amy Noelle Parks
Hardcover edition first published in the United States of America
in 2021 by Albert Whitman & Company
Paperback edition first published in the United States of America in
2022 by Albert Whitman & Company
ISBN 978-0-8075-7670-0 (paperback)
ISBN 978-0-8075-7661-8 (ebook)

Printed in the United States of America
10 9 8 7 6 5 4 3 2 1 LB 26 25 24 23 22 21

Cover art copyright © 2021 by Albert Whitman & Company
Cover art by Jensen Perehudoff

For more information about Albert Whitman & Company,
visit our website at www.albertwhitman.com.

For my mom and dad, who made me brave

CHAPTER 1

Summer Wish

Knox, Vivi, and I lie flat on our backs like spokes on a wheel, each with a dandelion in one hand. It's the last day of seventh grade, and we're about to make our Summer Wish.

"Close your eyes," Vivi says.

I obey.

Knox huffs in protest. "I have *got* to get some guy friends." He's mostly a good sport, but sometimes he complains that Vivi and I girl out on him.

"You have Colby," I say.

"Only because he doesn't know I do this stuff with you two."

"Shh," Vivi says as the bell tower tolls. When the last of the five clangs fades, I purse my lips and blow. The wind catches a few seeds and lifts them up into the bright-blue sky, where they swirl about with the ones blown by Knox and Vivi.

"Time!" Vivi says. She sits up and tosses empty containers to us. Because of her nine-month-old sister, Vivi's house has an endless supply of baby food jars. Vivi claimed them for our summer ritual so we don't fill up more landfills with plastic bags. I stuff my dandelion stem in and twist the lid. Vivi does the same, but Knox stays on his back, twirling his stem in his fingers.

"No cheating," Vivi says, plucking the dandelion out of his hand and trapping it inside the jar.

"How'd we do?" he asks.

"Bakery," Vivi answers.

Vivi and I leap up, but Knox stays on the ground, eyes closed. He's always either moving or half-asleep, and it's hard to get him to go from one to the other. Vivi and I each take an arm and pull him to his feet.

"Don't you want to see who won?" I ask.

"It's always Vivi. Blowing dandelions is her superpower."

Vivi shakes her dark, blue-tipped ponytail. "Neither of you actually wants to win. Lilla doesn't even try."

This is true. Too much pressure.

I like starting our summers this way because of the tradition, but I'm not as into winning as Vivi and Knox.

Our game began when we were seven. Vivi and I were walking home on the last day of second grade, and I gave her a dandelion and told her to make a wish, but Vivi, being Vivi, turned wish-making into a competitive sport.

It started with counting pips. Vivi said whoever blew off the most seeds would be the winner—the one whose wish was most likely to come true. But two years later, Vivi and Knox decided we couldn't trust fate (and blowing) to get what we wanted. So we added a new rule: whoever had the fewest seeds left on their stem got to make an epic wish for the summer, and the losers had to make it come true.

Vivi won (of course) and wished for the Summer of the Lemonade Stand. We set up across the street from the college campus, and I made enough money that Mom and Dad opened a bank account for me because they said it was too much to keep in my cat purse.

When Knox won at the end of fifth grade, he demanded a trophy to give to the person who carried out his wish the best. We claimed a golden bowling ball with little tennis shoes and a goofy grin that Vivi's parents got at some kind of ironic bowling party. I'd never admit this to Vivi or Knox, but I love its cheerful little face. Not enough to fight to keep it though.

Vivi and Knox rush ahead toward the bakery to start counting seeds, but I'm caught by the golden afternoon light peeking through the pale-green leaves. I pull out my sketchbook, not worried about keeping up.

I've gotten used to walking on my own.

When I lived on the same street as Knox and Vivi, we went home through campus together almost every day. Vivi's and my parents work here, and so does Knox's mom, so the college campus has always been our playground. We went to day care at the lab school, learned to swim in the pool, had picnics in the commons, and one time knocked over a bunch of college kids when we went sledding down the main walkway in the middle of winter.

I'm not here quite as often now because last year my parents moved to a neighborhood of smushed-together duplexes on the other side of the college. Sometimes Vivi and Knox still walk with me, pretending it's on their way, but it's not. This will only be a problem for one more year, because all of us will ride the bus for high school. Wherever we end up.

Our county has two high schools: Morningside, that's the "regular" high school, and Grover Academy, a little magnet school where you focus on either the arts or math-science sorts of things. Grover Academy uses your seventh-grade test scores to decide if you're good enough to even apply, and we should find out if we hit the cutoffs any day now.

Knox grabs my hand, yanking me out of my thoughts. "You fell behind. You didn't hear a word we said, did you?" His brown eyes crinkle at the corners.

Vivi's eyes are laughing too. "You know we share Lilla with her imaginary friends. It was their turn to talk."

4

This is an old joke, and I scowl only because she wants me to. "What did I miss?"

"What we're going to make you do for the Summer Wish." Vivi snaps her gum. "Knox wants a physical challenge, but I'm planning psychological warfare."

"You're both mean."

"And you're a pushover," Vivi says. "It's our job to toughen you up."

This is the story of us. Vivi is the firecracker. Knox is the joker. And I am the good girl. Which is another way of saying I'm not very interesting.

Vivi always wants Summer Wishes that are good for us. Last year, she did the Summer of Learning a Language, a challenge Knox and I had to admit was fair, since Vivi speaks three languages, and he and I are white kids from the Midwest who only know one. We wanted her to teach us Japanese—which she knows because of her dad, but, honestly, Vivi is a terrible teacher. Everything comes so easily to her that she got mad when we didn't catch on. But Vivi's mom is French Canadian and was on bed rest because of her pregnancy, so she was happy to take over our lessons if we switched to French. It ended up being my favorite Summer Wish, even though I can mostly only say that the ocean is big and that I would like to take a taxi to the airport. (Since I have never actually been in a taxi, it's not all that useful.)

When Knox got to pick the wish, he was completely

ridiculous. During his Summer of Toothpick Ninjas, Vivi and I had to try to sneak a toothpick into someone's shoe every day. While they were wearing it.

I spent the summer chucking toothpicks at people's feet and hoping for the best. Vivi easily won the trophy, but I did earn bonus points by getting a toothpick into Knox's red Converse sneakers three separate times.

I've never made the Summer Wish. I'm not really sure what I'd ask for if I won. Maybe the Summer of No Arguing. But I've learned that's not the kind of thing you can make true with a wish.

Knox and Vivi are up ahead, waiting by the door of Cookie Mistake, the on-campus bakery that sells less-than-perfect desserts made by students in the culinary program.

When we enter, the manager, who's known us since we were in preschool, says, "Hey, kids. Not much left today."

Knox picks up a small, lopsided, chocolate layer cake.

"For all of us?" Vivi asks.

Knox hugs the cake to his chest. "It's only a little one."

Vivi and I share a smile. Over the last year, we've gotten used to this new appetite of his. I'm pretty sure he turns chocolate directly into height.

Vivi and I split a giant, underbaked cookie and eat it while we count dandelion seeds. By the time I finish, she's drumming her fingers on the table.

When I look up, she says, "Thirty-three!"

Her all-time record low.

Knox sighs. "Fifty-six." Then he forks a giant bite of cake into his mouth. They both look at me.

"Ninety-eight," I admit.

"At least she's under a hundred this year," Knox says. "It's almost like she tried."

"I try."

"No, Lilla, you don't," Vivi says. "But that's your bad luck."

"Viv," I say, trying to put the brakes on any extreme ideas. Summer Wish or not, I'm not going to let her make me do anything I don't want to. But I'm also not great at saying no.

"Well," Knox says to Vivi, taking a break from his cake eating, "what's your diabolical plan?"

"I wish for you two to be brave."

"What does that mean?" I ask. Last summer, she wanted to go horseback riding, but when I saw how big those animals were, I couldn't make myself do it. "Nothing dangerous, right?"

Vivi shakes her head. "You know I wouldn't do that."

I give her a look.

"Not as part of the Summer Wish," she adds. "*I* take it seriously." She passes the look I gave her on to Knox.

"Hey," he says. "Putting toothpicks in strangers' shoes was brave."

Vivi rolls her eyes. "I'm not talking about stuff like that. I mean really brave. Like doing something you're scared of or telling the total truth even if someone might not like it, or trying something new."

Knox points his fork at Vivi. "I don't think you want the total truth from me."

Vivi steals the cake from his fork. "I'm not saying you should tell us every disturbing thought in your scary boy head."

Knox grins. Something in his smile makes me wonder what he's hiding.

"But one way or another, you're both doing this," Vivi says. "It's our Summer of Brave!"

CHAPTER 2

White Lies and Silences

"What if, instead, it was our Summer of Ice Cream?" I ask.

Vivi narrows her eyes and Knox laughs.

I want to play fair. I really do. Even if I haven't loved every wish, I love this tradition. But right now is not a good time to be brave—for me or for Knox. "You know what it's like for us."

Knox nods. "If you want brave, I'll parasail or eat at that hot dog place with the weird bugs on the walls or get onstage and sing," he tells Vivi. "And except for a scary boy thought or two, I can tell you and Lilla about most stuff. But not my parents. It's not a game for me."

Knox's parents got divorced when we were nine, two years before mine split up. His family's divorce was ugly, with lots of shouting and fighting about custody. The judge made

Knox pick who he wanted to live with most of the time, and he feels like his dad never forgave him. His parents still yell when they see each other and are always asking Knox to pass on snarky messages. For Knox, flying under his parents' radar is a way of life.

It's a little different with Mom and Dad, who believe in Child-Centered Divorce. (They say this a lot.) From what I can tell, this mostly means they ask if I'm okay a billion times a day.

But the only way I will be okay is if things go back to the way they were. Because even if they got back together—and I know, because I am not a kid anymore, this will not happen, but even if it did—it wouldn't be the same. Another family bought our house, and now they get to live on the same block as Vivi and Knox. So when my parents ask, I say I'm fine.

Because what's the point?

Knox meets my eyes, and I know he's thinking the same thing. Being honest with our parents is not going to make our lives better. It's going to make them more complicated.

Vivi reaches across the table for our hands. "I really think this could be good. For both of you."

"Viv, you sound like you're trying to fix us," Knox says.

Vivi's father is a psychologist. Sometimes I think she talks about us at the dinner table and comes back with a plan. It's not my favorite thing about her.

"I'm not trying to fix you, but I want the Summer Wish to mean something. It's not supposed to be silly."

Vivi and Knox glare at each other long enough to worry me. "I'll do it," I say. "As long as there are no horses."

Vivi squeezes my hand. "We can start small. The first challenge can be honesty. Keep track of how often you lie."

After a moment, Knox says, "Fine. I'm going to my dad's this weekend. It'll give me something to do."

"I don't lie very much," I say. And I mean it. I always tell my parents where I'm going and who I'm with. I've never exaggerated a grade or even taken a cookie when I'm not supposed to. "I'll never beat Knox."

"There's all kinds of ways to lie," Vivi says.

"What's that supposed to mean?" I ask.

"White lies and silences count. And those are your specialty."

"Silence isn't a lie. I'm a quiet person."

"Sure," Vivi says. "But a lot of the time you're quiet because you're afraid. Afraid someone will be angry or will disagree or won't think you're the sweetest thing going."

"Because I am the sweetest thing going," I say.

"She has a point," Knox says, licking the frosting off his fork.

"Thank you," I say.

"I meant Vivi," he says with a smile.

It's not exactly news that Vivi thinks I keep too much to myself. She wishes I would talk more about everything— the divorce, boys, my grades, even my period. But I didn't know Knox wanted me to be more open too. Do they think I would lie…to them?

I mean, sure, there are things I haven't told them. I get bored watching their soccer games sometimes. And I actually did want to take baking as one of my electives last year instead of doing outdoor explorers with the two of them. And, no, I did not think that video of the dog eating watermelon was so funny that I wanted to watch it over and over again. But so what if I kept these thoughts to myself? It's called *being nice.*

I don't make things up. I'm just a little…careful.

"So you want me to keep track of all my white lies and silences?" I'm still trying to understand the rules. "If I have more than Knox, will I win?"

"Ah, no. That's not it at all," Vivi says. "It's just I don't think you two even know how much you lie—or keep to yourselves. This challenge is about being brave enough to see what you're doing…that's what I'm grading."

"Okay," I say, turning to Knox.

He shrugs. "It's her Summer Wish. But I just want to point out that if I'd won, we'd be having the Summer of Hitting Buses with Water Balloons, and it would be a lot more fun."

When we leave the bakery, Vivi and Knox turn to walk with me, but I shake my head. "Don't be silly. It's the complete opposite direction."

"I'm not in a hurry," Vivi says.

"No," I say. Having them with me makes it worse because it reminds me of how different everything is. "I think I can find my way without the two of you holding my hand."

"That's not what I meant," Vivi says. She knows I'm a little touchy about the way they baby me sometimes.

"I know, but it's fine."

"You're sure?" Knox says. Ever since I moved, they insist on walking me home if it starts to get even the littlest bit dark, but really, what's going to happen to me in the broad daylight?

"Get out of here," I tell them. I don't want them feeling sorry for me because I have to go off on my own, so I smile and wave.

Maybe Vivi will give me extra points for this whole new kind of lie: the nonverbal.

*

Honestly, I like walking on my own. I like being able to stop and sketch a tree without anyone waiting for me, or to think about a book I'm reading without getting interrupted, but I do wish I was walking toward my old house.

There's nothing wrong with our new place. It's a tall, narrow duplex painted pale blue with scallopy white trim. My upstairs bedroom has a balcony out back. And it's a two-minute walk to school, which was nice this winter.

But it's pretty weird.

Mom and Dad bought the house because they didn't want me moving back and forth between them after the divorce. But I still do—it's just the trip is pretty quick since I only have to go up and down the back stairs. Mom lives in the upstairs apartment. Dad lives in the downstairs one. I live in both.

Or neither. It depends how you look at it, I guess.

This setup is called "bird-nesting." They read about it in some magazine. Usually it means the kid stays in the same house (or nest) all the time, and the parents move in and out (like birds, I guess). But Mom and Dad say it's easier to have a duplex and have me move back and forth.

They did not like it when I asked easier for who.

Mom and Dad say they are Committed Co-parents who put my needs in front of theirs. When they say this, you can tell they are very proud of themselves. But if they actually thought my needs were as important as theirs, bird-nesting wouldn't be necessary, would it?

Even though I don't have to move back and forth across town like Knox, the book I'm reading and the sweater I want and my sketchbook are always in the bedroom I'm not in.

Mom and Dad say the whole thing is a fair way to share custody.

Even before the divorce, Mom and Dad were big on fair. They divided up my name. Dad picked Lilla for the painter

Lydia Cabot Perry. Mom chose Edith for Edith Patch, the first woman president of the Entomological Society of America. Baxter is Mom's last name, and Willoughby is Dad's. Lydia "Lilla" Edith Baxter-Willoughby. It's a lot of name, but there's something for everyone.

My activities are also evenly split. When Mom signed me up for Girls Who Code, Dad put me in a drawing class. I like computers and art, but sometimes I wish everything didn't have to be so balanced. It's like my whole personality is a popularity contest.

Three nights a week, I eat dinner with Mom, and three nights I eat with Dad. The seventh night we go out as a family, so I can feel secure and not grow up to do something terrible because of the divorce, like shoplift or not get into a good college.

They think I'm fine with all this. And I try to keep it that way. Even when I want to, I make sure not to shut myself in my room. Either one of them.

And I do not cry at the dinner table. Because that is what therapy is for, and Dad says I should not manipulate people with my tears.

I don't complain when I have to walk downstairs for my phone charger, because lots of girls my age don't even have phone chargers.

It's true that one time I underlined the part of the article about bird-nesting that said the child gets to stay in one place.

Mom and Dad said this was not giving them the Credit They Deserved. They say I should be grateful they don't shout all the time like Knox's parents or force me to choose between them or make me live far away from my school. They have worked hard to make this easy for me, so the least I can do is Appreciate Their Efforts because this bird-nesting thing is not so fun for anyone.

Mom and Dad say they got divorced because they weren't happy. I didn't even know you could do that. I thought you got divorced if someone did something terrible or if you screamed and yelled all the time. I thought if you weren't happy, you got a hobby. Or therapy. Or meds.

Not a bird's nest.

So now, even though it's hard sometimes, I do all I can to keep them happy. Because if they're not, who knows what they'll do next.

CHAPTER 3

Choices

The door on the left side of our duplex is open behind the screen. Dad's door is closed up tight, so he's probably not home. Which is fine. It's Mom's day anyway. I trot up the stairs, because the faster you move, the happier you sound.

"Welcome home, eighth-grader!" Mom calls.

"Smells good," I say as I come into the kitchen.

"Grilled cheese with cinnamon apples." This is our favorite sandwich, and we eat it all the time. It's one of the good things about the divorce.

Dad says sandwiches are not an appropriate dinner. He likes to cook fancy meals and grow his own vegetables and make furniture in the basement and write and read and go to art museums.

Mom's more focused. She likes me. And bugs. And people

who study bugs. And that's about it. A few years ago, she got to combine all her favorite things on a trip to Ecuador. She discovered a new kind of wasp and named it after me—the *Aleiodes lilliae*. It's a little bit blue and sort of pretty. It could have been worse.

"Letter on the table for you," she says, grabbing plates for dinner. Her forced No-Big-Deal tone lets me know what it is: my end-of-grade test scores.

Even if my numbers are good, I'll have to go through Summer Showcase, where you prove how good you are at math or coding or drawing or whatever. Because school smart isn't enough. To get into Grover Academy, you have to be creative and curious and original.

And those are only the adjectives I remember. There's a whole list.

The competition to get in is bonkers. Living in a college town, a lot of us have professors for parents, and whatever the prize, they want their kids to win. And like a lot of parents, Mom and Dad also like to pretend they don't care. "She pushes *herself*," they say to anyone who will listen.

I flip the envelope over in my hand. There's no clue in its weight. My scores will be printed on a single sheet of paper.

To apply to the arts track, you have to test above the benchmark in English language arts, and for STEM, you have to do it in math. Mom and Dad disagree about which track I should focus on in high school. But they share a love for high test scores.

Mom watches me closely. "You're allowed to retest in case of hardship. I can call for you."

She means we could tell them I didn't do well because of the divorce. But it's hard to see how another couple of months would make a difference anyway. Even if I get used to this bird-nest thing, my parents will still be divorced.

But then, it's not like anyone would believe my excuse anyway. The whole retest thing is just a way to get people to back off. I don't even blame the school. Parents around here are pretty scary.

Last year one girl got a retake because her parents said she was devastated by the death of her goldfish. A classmate of hers got his redo because he lost his swim meet the day before.

I keep looking at the back of the envelope, and Mom keeps not saying that it will be fine if my scores are low. Because it won't be.

Obviously.

"I can't stand it anymore. Open it!" she says finally. When I don't move, she adds, "Unless you want your dad?" Mom twists a towel in her hand. "Should we?"

She sounds so uncertain. This is not like her. Or at least it didn't used to be. But she's read so many books on divorce, and her browser history is a horror show of late-night-panic googling about everything that could go wrong for me. (I wasn't snooping when I found this—just trying to get some homework done without having to go downstairs to get my laptop.) Mom tries real hard to include Dad on important things, even when she doesn't want to. But I hate it when she asks me to weigh in on this stuff.

"I don't think he's home," I say. "The door was closed when I got here." Mom frowns and looks toward the clock on the stove. It's after six. Dad loves his routines, and it's past time to start cooking.

To distract her, I rip the envelope. The letter is a mess of red and green bars and arrows and numbers.

"Well?" Mom says, hands curled into fists. She's trying not to rip the paper out of my hands. I find what I'm looking for—ninety-eighth percentile in English language arts, ninety-sixth in math.

I didn't just hit the benchmarks. I sailed over them. I can't name the feeling rising up. Relief, maybe?

Mom grabs the paper out of my hands, gives it a quick glance, and laughs. "That face! I didn't know what to think." She pulls me in for a hug. "Sure, the math score's not perfect, but it's good enough. And we can always get you some tutoring over the summer."

I'd hoped once these scores came in, I could take a break. If the showcase goes all right, I'll be set—as long as I don't screw up too much in eighth grade. Colleges don't see your middle school grades, so it would be a good year to chill some.

But Mom is right. If I do the magnet school—especially the STEM track—it's going to be hard. I can't afford to fall behind.

It's real important to Mom that I do well in math. Coming up in the sciences was hard for her. She was one of only a few girls all along the way, and she's all excited for me to follow in her footsteps. She doesn't care if it's entomology—thank goodness—but she's always saying things like "So many girls get pushed out of science in middle school. We can't let that happen to you." She would have seen it as a Failure of All Feminism if I'd chosen yearbook as an elective instead of forensic science when we did our eighth-grade schedules a few weeks ago.

(Fun fact: Entomologists get consulted all the time to help solve crimes. Mom once identified a murderer by the flea in his hair.)

Mom turns over the paper. "There's an information session about Grover Academy on Tuesday night, and the showcase is a week after that. I suppose we should hear what they say before we decide on your track. Make sure you're going to get in on the STEM side. But Elizabeth said her son got in with a ninety-two last year. You should be fine."

"Knox wants to do the arts program," I say. I'm not sure why. Testing the idea, maybe.

"Well, he has real musical talent, doesn't he?"

Which means my talent for drawing is what? I think. Imaginary?

We hear the downstairs door creak open, and our eyes meet. Mom's face goes a little sad, and she hands back the paper. "Go tell him. He'll want to know."

I nod and head downstairs, wondering for the infinitieth time whose idea this divorce was. In the beginning, it seemed like Mom was making everything happen, and Dad was as stunned as I was. But now, she's still sad, and he's happier and happier. I have no idea what caused it. All they'll say is that they aren't good partners for each other anymore, and it has nothing to do with me. I think they had to memorize this line in therapy.

The upstairs and downstairs apartments have separate doors on the front porch, but both have landings off the same wooden staircase in back. There's an attic on the top, a door to the outside on the bottom, and little round porthole windows all up the side.

I spend a lot of time reading out here. It's sunny and warm, and because it's an in-between space, it doesn't feel like it belongs to either Mom or Dad.

Dad lets me into his kitchen when I knock on the door. "Is it my night?" He looks over his shoulder at the stove. "I only bought enough for one."

I know he doesn't mean to make me feel unwanted. Even though Mom's the scientist and Dad's the art historian, he's way more literal than she is. He's just reporting the number of steaks in his kitchen. Still, I have to squash down my sadness. "No. Mom's making sandwiches."

I hold out my paper. "I got my test scores. She thought I should show you. I mean…I wanted to."

He takes the paper, making sense of it so much more quickly than I did. "Congratulations, Lydia Edith. I'm happy to see this." Not that you'd know it by looking at him. Dad and I have the same hazel eyes, light-brown hair, and soft features, but his face doesn't move around nearly as much as mine, because Dad doesn't show emotions. He narrates them.

This drives Mom batty. Or is it *drove*? Do things like this stop bothering you after a divorce?

"So, the higher English score means the arts track. You want to take the sure bet. Guarantee you get in." He doesn't make any of this a question.

"Makes sense." Is not telling him Mom thinks I'm doing the STEM track a white lie or a silence?

I'll figure it out later.

Deciding what to do for the showcase is stressful enough without my parents arguing over which track I should apply to. If I'd been really smart, I would have tanked one of the tests, so I only had one choice.

Or I could have blown both tests and had no way to get into Grover Academy. I'd have to go to Morningside. My mind leaps away from that thought like it's a hand over a hot stove. I want to go to the magnet school. Obviously. Why wouldn't I?

I missed some of what Dad said, but he seems to be explaining the rules. "You get a five-by-ten space to display whatever you want. Let's go through your portfolio tomorrow. We'll figure out what we can use, and if you need to do something new."

He means *he* will figure it out.

Dad flips the paper over. "And we have to go to a meeting Tuesday. The arts one is at seven."

Uh-oh. "It's not one big meeting?"

Looking at the paper, he shakes his head. "No. First STEM and then the arts. Isn't that always the way?" He looks up at the ceiling. "Do you need me to talk to her? Is she disappointed about your choice?"

My choice.

Even with his blank face, it's pretty easy to see Dad would rather do anything other than go upstairs and explain to his ex-wife that her daughter would rather draw than do science.

"Maybe I could go to the arts one with you and the science one with her?" I suggest.

He tilts his head, thinking about it. "Sure. That could work. Like you're considering both."

"Yeah," I say. "Like that."

CHAPTER 4

Myself, But More

Over the next two days, the breezy little thought that float-
ed through my mind when I got my test scores grows into
a hurricane.

The more I chase away the idea, the more it pops up.
When I go to bed. When I wake up. In my loopy hand-
writing under the self-portrait in my sketchbook. I try it
on for size.

I don't want to go to the magnet school.

Looking at the page, I whisper it. Lightning doesn't crack
across the sky, and the walls of my room don't shake. I'm a
little surprised.

Turning down the magnet school is not something professors' kids do. We never even talked about *whether* I would
go. As long as I can remember, going to Grover Academy

was the thing I would do before college. The school's reputation was part of why Mom and Dad took jobs here in the first place.

Sometimes, they did talk about what would happen if I didn't get in. Their backup plan was tutoring and retesting so I could transfer in later.

Dad says it's where you graduate that matters, not where you start. He grew up in the middle of nowhere and did two years of community college after high school. Even before things got bad, he used to make a lot of little comments about the fancy schools Mom went to.

Of course, that doesn't stop him from wanting them for me.

Maybe I've watched one too many movies, but I want high school to be more than choosing between AP Art and AP Chem. I want to go to football games on Friday nights and art club and Odyssey of the Mind.

And—I feel like I have to whisper this thought even in my head—maybe I want a school where everyone doesn't know me as the girl who follows Vivi and Knox around.

They're both so sure of what they want. Knox never looks more like Knox than when he plays the guitar, and Vivi's the same when she codes. I can see her next to me finding pathways two and three steps ahead. If I talk to her when she's in the middle of it, she jumps right out of her seat.

Sometimes I wonder if something's wrong with me because

I don't feel like that about anything. I like coding and drawing and writing and solving equations. But not the way they
do. I'm not even sure I'd want something to take me over
like that.

My phone buzzes.

Vivi: Summer Wish check-in!

Lilla: Only 3 lies. I told you. Very honest.

Vivi: And white lies?

Lilla: *sigh* 16. It's their fault. They keep asking me questions.

Vivi: Oh, well *questions.* Who can blame you?

Lilla: And before you ask, there's lots of silences too. I don't
know how many.

Vivi: Because you can't count that high.

Lilla: Harsh. Do I win the first round?

Vivi: Depends on how complete your journal is. Knox wrote a
song about lying to his dad. So pressure's on. See you after your
interview tomorrow?

Lilla: I'll find you.

Vivi: Good luck!

Vivi, Knox, and I applied to be junior counselors for the
summer camps run by the three museums on campus. My
cousin Sara says I'm extra for wanting a summer job while
I'm still in middle school. And I get it. Part of me likes the
idea of spending my whole summer swimming.

But summers by the pool aren't so much the vibe in our
town. Here, kids go to orchestra camp so they can finally

take down that girl who beat them out for first chair the last two years, or they travel to other countries to brush up on their second (or third) language, or they take math classes at the college so they can get to calculus as sophomores and then do who knows what their last two years of high school.

If I said I wanted to lie around by the pool all summer, my parents would send me right back into counseling because they'd worry the divorce led to a Lack of Ambition.

Besides, I've always loved the museum camps. Junior counselor is first step to being hired as a real counselor when you're sixteen, and that would be a pretty awesome summer job.

Because Dad is the director of the art museum, I basically grew up inside the giant building that houses the museums. I learned to draw by copying paintings, and I spent hours in the science museum looking at fossils, giant beehives, and models of the lunar surface, but the children's museum has always been my favorite.

You can race boats through a maze of waterways and build a Rube Goldberg machine and work in a pretend grocery store with carts and a cash register and a conveyor belt that moves when you press a button with your foot. There's a giant pirate ship you can climb on and a tree house with a reading nook.

I'm too old for all of it, but if I get picked as a junior counselor, I'm totally building a fort with the giant foam blocks. Knox and I tried the last time we were there, but little kids kept taking our blocks and looked like they'd cry if we took them back.

They only pick six kids across the three museums, and they'll for sure put Vivi in the science camp. And Knox is perfect for the children's museum. He plays the guitar and the piano and makes up games all the time. I'm not as sparkly as they are, but I think I'd be good at working with shyer kids. I hope I can make them see that.

Mom pokes her head in the door, taking in the pile of clothes on my bed. "What's all this?"

"Figuring out what to wear tomorrow."

She sits down and picks up a black dress with little white polka dots. "This is perfect," she says. "Mature, but age-appropriate."

"I was thinking the orange skirt." I hold it up. "The camp's for kids…so something fun?"

"It's up to you, but you want to be taken seriously. That's important for girls."

"I'll wear the black."

"Good choice. Have you thought about what you're going to say?"

I shrug. "Not really. I don't know what they're going to ask."

"But you can guess. Why you want to do this. What experiences you've had that will help. You need to show them who you are. Demonstrate passion."

"Sure."

"But don't be overemotional."

"Got it." To me, my voice says, "We're done here," but Mom seems to hear it as "Please, tell me more."

"Be yourself. See if you can let your test scores slip. That will help."

I nod.

"Talk about your science fair project, and how much you loved that paleontology camp. And your babysitting too."

"Sure. My passions," I say.

"Absolutely. And watch your language. Rein in those 'reallys' and 'totallys.'"

"Myself. But more."

"Exactly."

This is our family motto.

CHAPTER 5

Life Skills

The next morning, I walk to the museum with Dad.

At the door, he gives me a quick hug. "Do you me want to…" His voice trails off.

I nod. Everyone will know I'm my dad's daughter, but we don't have to make a big deal of it. I let him go toward the employee entrance before I walk through the area that connects the three museums.

There's a classroom in the back with floor-to-ceiling windows. A sign on the door says, "Welcome, future junior counselors!" I check my phone. Ten minutes early. I fuss with the straps on my sandals. I have no idea how I'm supposed to do this. Will someone come out? Should I go knock? Nine minutes. Maybe I should have had Dad stay with me?

I go to the drinking fountain. From there, I can check out

the classroom without being obvious. A woman, a little younger than my parents, lays out art supplies on the table, making the room look more like a birthday party than a job interview. Her blond hair is up in a ponytail, and she's wearing a bright-pink flowered dress. My orange skirt would have been fine. I sort of want to take a picture to show Mom, but probably taking pictures of the person interviewing you is weird.

Three minutes before nine o'clock, I go to the door. The woman doesn't notice me, so I back up and try again, stomping my feet a little this time. When she hears me, the woman looks up and smiles. She holds out her hand. I take it and squeeze. This is a completely normal thing to do, but I can't remember if I've ever shaken someone's hand. It seems weird that with all the totally useless things I've learned in school, no one ever had me practice this.

"I'm Kate Krause, and I'll be running the camps this summer. You're Lilla?"

"Yes," I agree. My voice is too quiet. I give a big smile to make myself seem louder. And bigger, I guess.

She smiles back. "Why don't you have a seat?"

Kate asks why I'm interested in being a junior counselor. I talk about how much I've loved the camps I've done at the museum, keeping secret my plans to build a block fortress. This must work because Kate tells me I am a Mature Young Lady. Mom would not like this. She thinks *lady* is an insult.

"Okay. Hands-on part next," Kate says. "I'm going to leave

the room for fifteen minutes. I want you to plan a camp activity using the things in this room."

Whoa. I definitely did not expect this. And neither did Mom.

The table's full of art supplies—markers, scissors, craft feathers, straws, cardboard tubes, and popsicle sticks. Maybe musical instruments? But I always hated being told exactly what to do when I was at camp, and it's super hard to get little kids to follow directions.

Looking for ideas, I run my hands along the spines of the books at the back of the room. One on hot-air balloons catches my eye. I pull it out and find some others on planes, blimps, butterflies, and birds. Then I stand them up on the table and sort the art supplies so they look more inviting.

"Want to tell me about this?" Kate says when she returns.

I explain my idea: invite kids to make their own museum exhibit about flying machines.

Kate nods. "Well done. Open-ended is important. Lots of people don't get that."

"Thanks," I say, feeling like I passed a test without knowing what was being graded.

"Let's say you're doing this, and a six-year-old asks how planes fly. What would you say?" Kate looks like she can't wait to hear whatever fabulous thing comes out of my mouth, which I suspect had better not be: look it up on my phone.

I remember sticking my hand out the car window and feeling it get pushed up and down when I tilted it in different directions. I share this with Kate. Then I panic.

"Wait. Was that a terrible answer? Is it bad to tell a kid to stick her hand out of a moving car?"

She laughs. "No. Bad happened last year when one of our senior counselors answered a physics question by saying 'magic.' You want to see parents in this town flip out, go all anti-science on them. Most of them are willing to risk a broken finger or two if it'll teach their kid something."

I nod, because that seems about right. If she wants science, I can give her a little more. I hand Kate a strip of construction paper.

"Hold it to your lips." I show her with mine, and she copies me. Our paper strips flop down in front of us like giant lizard tongues.

"Now blow across the top," I say.

She does and the paper strip rises in front of her. Amazed, she looks at me. "Why did that happen?"

"Lift. Like an airplane wing. The air blowing across the top shields the paper from the air pushing down, but the air underneath is still pressing up. So the paper rises. That's what happens when a plane goes fast and wind blows across the top of the wing."

"Clever," she says. "I don't normally do this at the interview, but how would you like to be one of our junior counselors?"

"Really?"

"Yeah. You did great. Is the science museum good? We

don't get many girls we can put into that role." That's a surprise. My advanced science class at school is at least half girls.

I wonder if I actually have a choice. I want to play in the grocery store and put on puppet shows and chase bubbles in the children's museum. But it seems safer not to argue.

Mom will be happy with this. And Vivi. We can work together.

So I smile and say, "That sounds great."

"Okay. I'll be in touch with your parents tonight. We'll have a week of training before the camp. Your job is to help the high school students who will be our senior counselors."

"Will you let everyone know if they made it tonight?" I ask. If Vivi and Knox get in, we can celebrate.

"Not sure, but everyone will know by tomorrow morning at the latest."

"Well, thanks for not leaving me in suspense."

She slides a folder over to me. "Our handbook. There's a couple of things I want to go over. And a few forms for your parents to sign in the back."

Paging through the book, she tells me the camp hours and my responsibilities. The museum can't pay us until we're fifteen, but Kate says she's a judge for the Grover Academy Summer Showcase, and her junior counselors usually do well. She tells me she'll be judging visual arts, but that she can put in a good word for me in anything. I don't tell her that maybe I'd rather she didn't.

Then she flips to a page at the back of the handbook that says "Dress Code." There's a line down the middle. One column says "boys" at the top. The other says "girls." There are no other options.

The boy side has three rules: no vulgarity, no tank tops, no underwear showing over beltlines. The girl side has fifteen. The ones most important to me are: no leggings; all skirts and shorts must hit no more than three inches above the knees; and shirts must not be inappropriately tight.

I smooth my dress on my lap, wondering if the three inches is when I'm standing up or sitting down. I'm tempted to pull on my top too. What is *inappropriately tight*?

This whole list makes me feel like I did something wrong.

"Any questions?" Kate asks cheerily.

"Um, no leggings?" I ask. Leggings seem like they'd be good for getting down on the floor and making messes.

Kate smiles, like we're sharing a secret. "We want to focus on the kids."

I frown because that's what I'm trying to do.

"We don't need any distractions," she continues.

"Distractions?" I echo.

"You know how boys are."

I nod and smile because I want the job, but I don't see why boys have anything to do with what I wear to camp.

Kate pats my hand. "Trust me. It's easier this way."

CHAPTER 6

Commitment and Passion

Vivi and Knox have soccer camp every morning this week. I hurry home to change before heading to the fields to meet Vivi. Even in practice, she's fierce. Girls flinch when she moves in to take the ball.

Afterward, she runs over to me. "Thanks for coming!"

"No problem. Come over for lunch?"

"Grilled cheese and apples?" she asks.

"I bet we can talk my mom into it." Unlike some parents, Mom's totally okay with me eating the same thing over and over. She says there's more important things to think about than food.

"Great!" Vivi says, pulling out her phone. "Let me ask."

"And then I have to tell you something." I feel some kind of way about telling Vivi about the museum, but with everything she said about my silences and white lies, I feel like I have to.

"Okay," she says. "But let's say hi to Knox and Colby first. Colby got his hair cut. It's super cute!"

"Oh. Okay." It's fine, I think. She doesn't know what I have to say is important.

All this talking about boys being cute and who likes who and how you know if you have a crush is new. It's not that these things never cross my mind, but I don't want to say them out loud. It all feels ridiculous. Like we're characters on a Disney show instead of real-life friends.

When we come up to the field, Colby—whose hair is, I guess, more sticky-uppy than usual today—shouts my name and shoots a ball toward me, putting an alarming amount of force behind it. Before I can decide what to do, Vivi jumps in front me, traps it, and kicks it back.

"Pick on someone your own size."

Colby grins. Vivi's only an inch taller than me.

"Or at least pick on someone who plays," Vivi adds.

Colby gives me an apologetic smile. "Sorry. Forgot you don't do sports."

Irritated that he thinks my lack of soccer skills means I have no athletic ability at all, I take a few running steps and launch into an aerial. It's been a while, but it's pretty close to perfect, especially considering I'm on grass instead of a spring floor.

"Wow," he says.

"Don't underestimate Lilla," Knox says. "She's tougher than she looks."

"Maybe you should go back to gymnastics?" Vivi says. "You were so good."

I shrug. I don't want to talk about it. "It took a ton of time. And it was getting super expensive." This is the truth, but not the whole truth. (Does that make it a lie? Or a silence? Bravery-through-honesty turns out to be complicated as all get-out.)

My last two years in gymnastics I was at the gym every day and going to meets on weekends. I never saw Vivi or Knox and barely kept up with my schoolwork. And I wasn't like the other girls. It wasn't that they were better. Or at least not much. But they *loved* it. Came in early. Stayed late. Begged their parents to bring them to open gym on Sundays. Whatever spark they had, it wasn't in me.

Sometimes I miss it—that feeling of flight and of being a part of a group working toward the same thing. But mostly I'm happy to be free.

Neither Vivi or my parents get this. Vivi's all commitment and passion—for soccer and coding and math and manga. Mom and Dad could talk for hours—and painfully—about bugs and impressionist paintings. Even Knox would give up anything—even soccer—for music.

Maybe there's something like that waiting for me, but I haven't found it yet.

To change the subject, I say, "Guess what? I got hired as a junior counselor!"

"We're going to have so much fun!" Vivi squeals and throws her arms around me. "I mean, if I get it too."

We laugh. Of course she'll get hired. She's Vivi.

Knox messes with my hair.

"That's awesome," Colby says. "But how do you know? My interview's not till this afternoon."

"I guess I nailed the 'making things' part."

"The what?" Knox asks.

I tell them about the arts and crafts. Maybe it's not exactly fair, but Kate didn't tell me to keep it a secret, and these are my friends. Helping them makes it feel less like bragging.

"Thanks for the heads-up," Colby says. "I could use some good news."

"Why?" I ask.

"I got a big fat no on the magnet school. Just missed the cutoff scores. For both math and English." Colby laughs at my horrified expression. "It's okay," he adds. "It sucks, but it's not a major tragedy. For me anyway. My parents are devastated."

He says this like he thinks it's funny. But I can't imagine shrugging off Mom and Dad's disappointment so easily.

"It's because you're good at all different kinds of things," Vivi says. "The magnet school doesn't make sense for you."

Colby smiles at her. "I'll clean your cleats if you explain that to my mom."

CHAPTER 7

The Hard Stuff

We promise to meet Knox and Colby at the park to celebrate after everyone's interviews. Knox's dad missed his weekend with him and, as an apology, sent a giant package of paintballs that explode when you throw them at people. Both Knox's parents make tons of money. They like to say sorry with fancy presents, and Knox likes to share.

Sometimes, I wish both he and Vivi wanted to spend more time with just us, but mostly I'm grateful they drag me into things. I'd be alone in my room a lot more if it weren't for them.

When Vivi and I come into Mom's kitchen, Mom gets up from her laptop and gives me a big hug to congratulate me. I told her and Dad earlier on our group text. I try to make sure they find everything out at the same time.

Vivi looks at the computer. "What are you working on, Dr. B?"

"The usual. South American wasps."

"For what?" I ask. Mom doesn't normally teach in the summer.

"A little talk at Northwestern. Two nights next week. I put it on the calendar."

She motions toward the whiteboard on the fridge, where we track whether I'm sleeping upstairs or downstairs. Their schedules are too unpredictable for a regular routine, so the nights I'm at either place change all the time.

It's fine.

"Congratulations on your test scores, Vivi," Mom says, getting the panini maker out from the cabinet. "You and Lilla must be excited about high school."

"So excited," Vivi answers.

"And do you know what you're doing for the showcase?"

Vivi tells Mom about the computer program she wrote. She's all set.

"Maybe you can help Lilla?" Mom says. "She's dragging her feet."

"Have you decided between art and STEM?" Vivi asks.

Behind Mom I shake my head frantically.

"Oh, I don't think that part was much of a decision," Mom says. "We'll wait until the information night to make it official, but given her scores, why wouldn't she do STEM? She needs to get going on her exhibit though."

Vivi gives me a disappointed look. I shrug. She told me to keep track of my lies, not stop telling them.

To distract Mom, I point at her screen and say, "Isn't that my wasp? Why are you talking about old research?"

"It's sort of a highlight reel of my work."

"Is Lilla's your favorite insect?" Vivi says. "Because you discovered it?"

"Well, favorite's tricky." Mom sautés apples while she talks. "I love Lilla's wasp, but right now, given how important they are to our food supply and how under threat they are, it's hard not to have a soft spot for honeybees. And the *Chalcidoidea agaonidae* has always been a personal favorite. Without them we wouldn't have figs. Plus they have telescoping genitalia. So that's pretty great."

"Mom!" I say, horrified. "Don't say 'telescoping genitalia' to Vivi."

"She's very sensitive," Mom tells Vivi.

I roll my eyes and Vivi giggles. But really, what kind of mother doesn't just say, *Yes, the insect I named after my only daughter is my favorite?*

Mom puts the sandwiches on the grill.

"Is it hard to talk about that stuff? In public?" Vivi asks.

"Genitalia, do you mean?" Mom looks like she's trying not to laugh.

I can't believe I never thought to ask this. Because, yes,

I wish she'd bring it up less with my friends. But her work is about the mating habits of insects, so she must talk about this stuff all the time. And thinking about what our biology unit was like this year, I'd guess that must be hard sometimes. Like when she's the only woman in the room.

But she shakes her head. "Not really. I know it's hard to imagine, but boys do grow up some after middle school. The hard stuff is usually more subtle."

"Like what?" I ask.

"Getting interrupted, being called 'intuitive' instead of 'brilliant,' having men who study beetles explain wasps to me."

Thinking about this morning, I ask, "Are there rules about what you wear?"

"Like a dress code?" She laughs. "No. Although I think about it. You have to."

I guess this is the way it is. For me and Mom and Vivi anyway. I don't think Dad worries about his clothes. Or Knox.

"And it's not just about what you wear," Mom says.

"What else is it?" Vivi asks.

"Learning to move in a space like you belong there. Being willing to stand up for yourself."

"I can do that," Vivi says.

Mom smiles. "I know you can. It's this one I'm worried about." She squeezes my shoulder.

"Don't worry, Dr. B," Vivi says. "We're working on it."

CHAPTER 8

Confessions

Later in my room, Vivi flips through the pages of my sketchbook. I'm not sure how she'll rate my drawings about lies against Knox's song, but whatever she decides, she'll be sure it's the right decision. I wish I had that certainty. About anything.

"Wow," she says, looking at the drawings of Mom's and Dad's faces, surrounded by my words. "You wrote down more than I thought."

"It's not like I'm making up huge stories," I say, wanting to defend myself. "But my life is a lot right now."

Between keeping my parents happy and the pressure around the magnet school and juggling plans for the summer, I'm keeping a few things to myself, but I'm not a master criminal.

Vivi flips to the page where I tracked all the lies I told Dad and lets out a breath in a quiet laugh.

"What?"

"Really? You couldn't tell your dad you didn't like his artichokes?"

"He knows I like Mom's cooking better, even though food is so much more important to him. I didn't want to hurt his feelings."

"But now you have to eat artichokes," she says with a shudder. Vivi's a more adventurous eater than I am, but she's not a huge fan of cooked vegetables.

"I've done harder things." Although artichokes do turn out to be squashier than you'd think. Maybe I went a little overboard telling Dad how good they were with lemon juice. They were fun to draw though.

She stops on the pages from the Summer Wish. On the left is Vivi, about to blow her dandelion. "The Summer of Brave" written over her head. On the right is Knox, eyes closed, thick lashes on his cheeks, and the words *I have got to get more guy friends*.

Vivi and Knox are the people I draw best in the world. I can't even draw myself that well. "There aren't any lies on that page," I say. Something about the way she's looking at the drawing makes me edgy. If anything, their pictures are maybe a little too true.

"How'd you do this?" she asks. "Your eyes were closed."

I shrug. "I know you both. I didn't have to see."

Vivi's fingers trace the drawing of her own face. "No lies to me and Knox? None at all?"

"No," I say. Too quickly.

"Then what's going on with the showcase? You were weird with your mom."

Vivi has this sixth sense about me. Somehow, she knows there's more here than me not wanting to choose between art and science (and my mom and dad). My heart beats hard in my chest. Why is it so much worse to think about lying to Vivi than to my parents?

Maybe because they lied so many times in the months leading up to the divorce. "Everything's fine," they'd say. And after. "Nothing's going to change."

But Vivi tells the truth. She's going to be hurt and think it's about her. But how I feel about the Grover Academy isn't about her, or at least not very much. Maybe I would—a little bit—like to get out of her shadow.

"Lilla," she says, wanting me to talk. It's too late. She'll see right through anything I make up. "What aren't you telling me?"

If I can't say this to her, I will never, ever be able to do it with my parents. With a big breath, I take my journal back, unclip the pages I was hiding, and find the self-portrait with my confession underneath: *I don't want to go to the magnet school.* I turn it around to show it to her.

Vivi gasps. Which is a little bit satisfying.

"Why not?" she says.

My heart beats in rhythm with her wish. *Be brave. Be brave. Be brave.*

"I hate the idea of picking a side—giving up art or science. And I'm so tired of all the competition and the tests and the rankings. I just want that to stop. And—"

Vivi waits. When I don't speak, she prompts, "And?"

"And I sort of wonder what it would be like...to do school without you and Knox."

Vivi turns away from me.

"I'm sorry," I say, reaching for her. "I don't really mean it."

"Yes, you do."

I don't know if I do or if I don't. It's so hard for me to know my own feelings when I'm drowning in everyone else's.

"It's just something that crossed my mind," I say. "But it doesn't matter because I can't tell my parents I'm not going, and I want to be with you both. You know that."

This is so hard. Until my parents got divorced, I thought they would be there. Together. Always. And then they weren't, and I had to put my life together without that.

The divorce taught me it's a mistake to count on anything or anyone. And so, what does it mean that I can't imagine walking into a cafeteria and finding somewhere to sit without Vivi or Knox? Or how to pick classes without thinking about what they're going to do first? I don't want to do high school without Vivi and Knox, but I'm starting to wonder if I need to.

"You and Knox are so…big. And you've made everything easy for me. But someday—even if it's not now—I'm going to have to figure out how to live without you two leading the way."

"I'm sorry if we're too pushy," Vivi says.

"You're not," I say. "But I think I rely on you too much. I don't even know if I could go to school without you. I probably wouldn't have even said anything if you hadn't asked me what I was hiding from Mom."

"That doesn't make me feel better," Vivi says. "Would you really have hidden this from me?"

"No. I mean, I don't know. It doesn't matter. I'm not going to do anything. My sketchbook is just…thoughts."

"Because your plan is to compete to get into this school you don't even want to go to so you can make your mom and your dad and Knox and me happy. This is how you're going to live your life?"

"Yes."

Vivi gives me a disappointed look.

I don't know why she's surprised. This is how I've always lived my life. "It's not like it would be terrible to go to Grover," I say. "I'd be selfish not to want that."

Saying any of this to Mom would send her right back to all those Nightmare on Divorce Street stories on the

Internet. I don't want her to blame herself because I'm not good enough. Or be embarrassed to tell her friends about me. I'd rather go to the magnet school.

And Dad. He wouldn't understand one bit of this. For him, it would be me throwing away this chance he never had growing up in his little farm town. Entitled. Unwilling to work. Without ever raising his voice, he'd guilt me into going.

"I can't tell them any of this. They wouldn't understand."

"You can. If this is really what you want, you have to tell your parents. And Knox."

"You're not the boss of me," I say, trying to make her smile.

"But I am." Before she would have said this proudly, but now she seems a little embarrassed. "The Summer Wish says so. If you'd blown on your dandelion a little harder, maybe we'd be having the Summer of Tea Parties, and you'd be judging our ability to put together cute cucumber sandwiches—I would win, obviously—but you didn't, so you're stuck. Unless...unless you don't want to do the Summer Wish anymore? You don't have to. I know I take over sometimes."

"Vivi, of course I want to do the Summer Wish," I tell her.

She looks unsure. It's scary seeing that expression on her face. I'm so, so sorry I said anything. If this is what comes from being honest, I don't want any part of it.

Vivi sighs. "Well, the good news is you beat Knox in round one. His song was cool and all, but his lies are nothing compared to what you've got going on here."

This does not make me feel better.

Vivi picks up my journal and thumbs the pages, as if she's looking for something in particular. "You're sure you're not hiding anything else? No other reason you want to go to Morningside?"

"What else could there be?"

"Anything, apparently."

She says this softly, but still, the words feel like a slap.

CHAPTER 9

Paintball Magnet

When Vivi and I meet later for Knox's paintball party, I ask how her museum interview went. She says, "I don't want to talk about it."

She's not over our fight earlier, but even with our Summer Wish, I'm not brave enough to call her on her silence.

Every single person is at the park. Knox, with his teams and his clubs and his bands, has tons of friends, and they're all here. When Knox sees us, he waves from the center of the crowd. High school without Knox and Vivi would definitely set the difficulty level higher. The idea of walking into a lunchroom without them almost makes me dizzy.

"How'd it go?" I ask Knox after the three of us move off some.

"Good. I brought my guitar and made instruments, and

Kate and I did a sing-along." I'm not surprised. Knox could charm someone a lot less perky than Kate.

"How 'bout you?" he asks Vivi.

"I don't think she liked me," she says. "She said my project would be too hard for the kids. But why does all that art stuff matter for the science camp anyway?"

So I guess Vivi does wants to talk about this, just with Knox.

"And she definitely didn't offer me a job right away."

"I'm sorry," I say. The last thing I need is for Vivi to be mad about this too.

"No one's blaming you," she answers. But it sounds like she is.

After looking back and forth between us, Knox says, "Luckily, we have the perfect distraction." He holds out a paper bag. "Four colors. Close your eyes, and pick a team. The rest are in buckets I hid across the creek."

I plunge my hand into the bag of squishy little globules. They feel like eyeballs. I pull my hand back.

"Don't be such a girl," Knox says.

"Hey!" Vivi says. She's got a blue paintball in her hand.

"Sorry," Knox says to her. And to me, "Don't be so Lilla-like."

"Fine," I say. This time I pinch one on top and pull it out. Green. "What does this mean?"

Knox grins. "That you're going down." He opens his hand to show another blue paintball. "Since me and Vivi are both blue, you can't hide behind us."

Knox passes the bag around to everyone else so they can pick their colors and climbs onto a rock to explain the rules. Then he plays a charging-trumpets sound on his phone, and everyone races for the creek. Vivi's out in front, but I hang back.

When I was seven, my family had a picnic here, and I was playing in this creek. I don't know what happened, because it's not like it's a regular thing, but all these leeches attached to my leg. They were bright pink and blubbery like that cranberry sauce that comes out of the can on Thanksgiving. When I brushed them off, they broke apart in my hands. It was so, so gross.

And so it doesn't matter how many kids I've seen come in and out of the creek leech-free, I am never, ever going in again, but it'll take me ten minutes to walk up over the bridge.

Knox bumps my shoulder. "Come on, Lil."

"You're not going to catch up with everyone?"

"Not without you."

"I'm going to take the bridge."

Knox knows the leech story. He pulls on my hand. "I'll protect you."

Following him down to the bank, I look suspiciously into the water. "How?"

The screams across the way die down as teams find their buckets.

Knox holds out his arms. "I can carry you."

"Are you sure?" I'm going to be upset if I end up in that water.

"It's not like you're person-sized."

"If you drop me, I will never speak to you again, Knox Donohue."

"Promises, promises."

I put my arms around his neck, and he scoops me up. When I lay my head against his chest, his heart beats in my ear.

How Knox smells is not a surprise—like detergent, a different brand from ours, and some kind of deodorant that probably has pine trees on the package, and chocolate. And I noticed before today he's gotten taller. And that his arms have these muscles you can see.

Until right now, these were facts about Knox. Like the way he eats entire cakes and plays the guitar and would rather read a book than solve a math problem.

But breathing in his particular Knox-scent while being held in his arms is doing something new. Odd little pulses leap in my chest. Like iron filings flying up to a magnet.

When Knox sets me down on the other side of the creek, I look for some sign of what I'm feeling in his face.

But he just gives me his usual smile—only not so usual, all of a sudden—and says, "You okay?"

Oh, no.

No, no, no.

I can't stop the thought: Knox is cute. His eyes and his freckles. And the way he tilts his head when he's confused.

"Lilla? Are you having leech PTSD?"

I shake my head, pressing my lips together because I'm afraid of what I might say.

He watches me for another couple of seconds and gives a puzzled smile. "Better run then. We're on opposite sides now." He takes off toward Vivi, who's waiting at the tree line.

She meets my eyes, but she's too far away for me to see what she's thinking. Hopefully that means she can't read my face either. Except that I'm sure my flushed cheeks can be seen from the space station. Cosmonauts are probably trying to scope out what's going on down here.

Colby shouts my name, and I follow his voice to the green bucket. I grab a couple of paintballs and hide in a little cave behind a bush. My best chance at winning is to stay hidden until everyone else gets picked off, and besides, I need a minute.

Crush doesn't come close to describing this feeling. *Whirl* or *flicker* maybe?

Do I like Knox? Like, like-like him?

I shake my head, embarrassed at the thought. I've read enough stories to have words for this, even if they aren't very good. But I can't believe I'm feeling it in real life. About Knox.

His laugh carries across the clearing. Easy to recognize. At least for me. Maybe his team won? With him and Vivi together, no one else has a chance.

I edge out of my hiding place and look around. Almost everyone is down by the riverbank, clearly already out.

I look toward where I heard Knox's laugh. He's peeking

around a tree, brown hair in his eyes. The urge to brush it out of his face surprises me, but not as much as the wet smack that hits my cheek a moment later. When I turn to see who hit me, I get nailed again on the shoulder. Then the stomach. Another ball flies past me and hits Vivek.

"Stop! I thought I only had to get hit once before I was out."

"Sorry!" Vivek says. "I was throwing before Vivi hit you."

"Me too," Sadie says. "But she got me too." Sadie has one little blue splatter on her hand. I'm pretty sure this is not what I look like. I turn back the other way.

Vivi lifts her shoulders apologetically. "Why were you just standing there with that goofy look on your face?"

I look toward Knox, who has bounded up. "I was wondering the same thing," he says. "You understood the point was not to get hit, right?"

I feel my cheeks heat. He saw me watching him. "I was trying to figure out what was going on."

"I was winning. That's what was going on," Vivi says.

"*We* were winning." Knox corrects. "It's a team sport, Vivian Tanaka." Somehow, the way he says her whole name makes them seem more connected than if he just called her Vivi.

I used his whole name before he carried me across the creek. Is this some kind of sign? When you like someone, do you start calling them by their first and last names? It makes a weird kind of sense because you get to hold their name in your mouth for longer.

But then he turns toward me. His smile gets bigger. My heart thumps.

"Lydia Edith Baxter-Willoughby, you are a mess. There ought to be a special award for getting hit by all the colors."

He said I was a mess. But he also called me all four of my names. I am a little bit thrilled by this. Also embarrassed. I've got a lot going on.

"There's no green," Vivi says, studying me.

"Look at the way the blue and yellow are running together on her neck. There's your green."

"Fair," Vivi says. She shakes her head. "Lilla, the paintball magnet."

When Knox goes off to say goodbye to everyone, Prisha comes over to offer me a packet of wet wipes.

"Wow, you were really prepared," I say. Prisha takes drawing with me, and I like her, but we don't spend a ton of time together—mostly because I'm usually with Knox and Vivi, and Vivi and Prisha don't get each other.

I had them both over once, but Vivi kept making little comments about the rom-coms Prisha wanted to watch and all the stuff she brought to do makeovers. Later, when I asked Vivi what her problem was, she said, "I'm just not into the whole Cotton Candy Princess thing she's got going on." But the thing is, I sort of am. I'm just not sure how to tell Vivi.

"Not my first rodeo," Prisha says.

Vivi presses her lips together. She's judging Prisha for

having a purse with wet wipes and caring about being dirty, but Vivi's not the one covered in paint.

"Thanks," I tell Prisha as I wipe my face.

Knox bounces up with Colby following. "Cookie Mistake?" he says hopefully.

"We can't go to the bakery like this," Vivi says. "We, in this case, meaning Lilla."

The worst of the paint is gone, but my arm is still stained blue. I can only imagine what my neck looks like.

"We could bring something out for you," Knox offers.

I shake my head. "I want to get cleaned up. You go ahead."

"I'll walk home with you," Prisha says. "It's on my way."

Vivi looks at Prisha and then at me. "If that's what you want?"

I can tell Vivi doesn't like this. Prisha's best friend moved away last year, and she thinks Prisha's auditioning me to take her place.

"You don't have to give up your cookie because I want a shower," I say. This is true. But it's also true that I want to talk to Prisha, so I feel guilty. "Check in tonight?"

Vivi's about to answer when Colby wipes his wet-paint-covered arm across Vivi's cheek and runs away. Vivi shakes her head and takes off after him. Knox waves and follows.

I go in the other direction with Prisha, trying not to feel like my choice means more than it does.

CHAPTER 10

Girled

As soon as we're on our own, Prisha says, "Can I ask you something?"

"I guess?" I say, worried it's going to be about Vivi. I like Prisha, but I'm not ready to tell all.

"How are you so good at noses?"

I laugh. Talking about drawing is a relief. "It's like anything else. You have to pay attention to the light and shadow. Not think about what they're supposed to look like."

She asks more questions about pencils and shading and blending stumps. It's fun to get all up in the detail of it. Vivi and Knox love my drawings but could not care less how they're made.

"Are you going to try for the arts program?" Prisha asks.

"I don't know." It might be nice to talk about this with

someone who isn't so worried about what I choose. We're at the corner of the elementary school where Prisha goes one direction and I go in the other, so I point to the playground. We each take a swing.

"Are you exhibiting?"

Prisha shakes her head. "Didn't make the cutoff."

"Oh. Sorry."

"It's okay. I didn't expect to."

It's hard to know what to say to this. Ever since we've been little, we've been sorted into these groups for reading and math, and no matter what they call them, we all know the rankings, but we mostly don't talk about them. I never thought about it before, but if I picture the table where I sit at lunch, it's all kids who have been in my reading group since third grade.

"Really, Lilla," Prisha says with a grin. "No biggie. I want to go to Morningside anyway."

She looks like she means this. And Colby didn't seem to care all that much either, even though he's always been in the advanced math groups with me and Vivi. I can't imagine being okay with not making the cutoffs. Even though I don't think I want to go, I'm glad I scored high enough to get in.

Because if I'm honest, part of the reason I'm afraid to say no to the magnet school is I don't want people to think I'm not smart. This is not a great look, I'm starting to see.

"I can't decide what to do," I tell Prisha.

"Why not exhibit and decide later? You'll have all year to change your mind if you get in."

"I mean I can't decide whether to try for STEM or art. I tested into both." I say the last part a little apologetically.

"Which do you like better?"

"Art, probably. But my mom thinks I should do science because there aren't enough girls and feminism."

"That's why my mom thinks I should stop cheerleading," Prisha says. "She says the whole point of Title Nine was to make sure girls could do 'real sports.'"

I wish everything wasn't so hard. That I could chose not to go to the magnet school without feeling like I'm letting down my whole gender. "Do you ever feel like there are too many rules for how to be a girl?"

"Are you kidding?" Prisha says. "My whole life is rules."

"Be smart, but don't show off," I say.

"Do well in school, but don't try too hard."

"Be pretty, but don't care about how you look."

"Be athletic—as long as it's soccer, softball, or field hockey—because cheerleading's too girlie and basketball isn't girlie enough."

"Tell the truth, but don't hurt anyone's feelings."

We're quiet for a minute, and I push back so I can swing up into the air. Prisha copies me.

Thinking about Kate's dress code, I say, "It's gotten worse lately."

"I know. All the rules felt different when we were kids. Maybe because I knew I'd outgrow them. But it seems like there's more every year." She leaps off the swing and I follow.

"Most people say 'girl' is a noun," I say. "But last year my English teacher said it's really a verb, and I think she's right. I keep getting *girled*. Mom and Vivi both seem so sure there's a right way to girl, and they don't think I'm doing it."

"But maybe there's more than one right way?"

"Maybe," I say. "But no one else seems to think so."

*

I take a quick shower upstairs with Mom's good shower gel. Then I head to Dad's because it's a downstairs night. Mom's not around, but I'm not surprised. She goes out a lot when I'm not here.

On my way down the back stairs, I hear voices. A man's and a woman's.

My stomach feels sick. I've seen Knox's parents date other people, so I knew this was coming. But still. I'm not ready. I'm not.

I sit on a step and think about what to do. The woman laughs. Only it's not a woman. It's Mom.

I slide down the stairs, and even though I know better, some wild *Parent Trap* stuff is swirling through my mind.

What does this mean?

I'm close enough now to see them sitting at Dad's kitchen table. Mom picks up a glass of wine and swirls it. "I miss this," she says. "You have to tell me what to buy. I'm so bad at it."

"I'll send you pictures of the labels."

Should I go in? Interrupting feels super awkward, and they'll stop talking if they see me. I'm really curious about what they're doing.

"That'd be nice." She looks at the table for a while. "So, should I do this?"

"Yes. You don't want to give this up. Again. That's how we ended up here in the first place. And you're not going to find something that works better. Not for a few years, anyway."

She nods. "Okay. And maybe it will make things easier for you."

"Not likely. When you're not here, Lilla is."

"When are you going to tell her?" Mom asks.

"I'm not. There's no one serious. What about you?"

"Not yet. She doesn't need to know unless it happens."

Shaking, I stand up. I thought I wanted to hear this, but I was wrong. I creep upstairs, planning to come back down loudly so they'll know I'm here, but on the way, a sob breaks through, and I run back into Mom's.

Lying on my bed with my door shut, I hear their words again and again. My divorced parents at a table, talking and laughing. Planning together. Keeping secrets.

From me.

Mom and Dad always say the divorce wasn't about me. But how can I believe that when what they want is to be left alone.

When you're not here, Lilla is. I can't stop hearing Dad's words. Talking about me like I am a burden. Like he wishes I was gone.

And so he can do what? Go out on dates with No One Serious? And not tell me, even though he keeps Mom—his divorced ex-wife—up to date.

And Mom? What is she not telling me? Does she have a No One Serious—or is it something worse? What would even be worse?

I stay on my bed for a long time—until Mom knocks on my door.

"Lilla? You're not supposed to be up here tonight."

Right, I think. I'm crying in the wrong bedroom. I tell her I'll be right down and sneak into the bathroom to wash my face with cold water.

Because I don't want to manipulate anyone with my tears.

CHAPTER 11

Upended

Dad and I make spaghetti Bolognese. He shows me how to chop onions, sauté meat, and break down canned tomatoes. At dinner, I ask what he's working on, and he talks about some Dutch impressionist paintings some guy found in his basement. They are going to revolutionize the way we think about brushstrokes or something. I don't know. I'm not really paying attention, but he's talking art, so he doesn't notice.

Afterward, we do the thing we always do. He asks if I'm okay. I tell I'm fine. He believes me.

I don't ask who he's dating. Or why he won't tell me. Or how he's going to see her when Mom goes wherever she's going.

I don't tell him that I heard their conversation. Or where I want to go to high school. Or that I'm so tired of moving back and forth between their apartments. Or that I might have a crush on one of my best friends and have no idea what to do about it.

Dad asks to see my portfolio. "You should probably go with your pencil drawings. Your portraits are strongest. Most original. But maybe one other? To show range? You can't just rely on your test scores. Talent matters too."

I look back at him. I could do it right now. Say what I want.

My mouth opens, but the words that come out are, "I'll go get my drawings."

After we finish, I text Vivi and Knox.

Lilla: You're right, Vivi. I need help.

Vivi: What are you talking about?

Lilla: I can't tell my parents anything.

Knox: Did you get hit in the head at paintball? Of course you can't tell your parents anything. They're parents. It's like the definition.

Vivi: You need practice. Try something easy first. Find out the world doesn't end because they're unhappy with you.

Lilla: Like the artichokes?

Vivi: Not that easy.

Knox: Artichokes?

Vivi: I'll come up with something.

Knox: I have a bad feeling about this.

Lilla: That's what you always say.

Knox: Someone has to.

A moment later, Vivi texts on our just-the-two-of-us chat.

Vivi: You okay?

Lilla: Not really.

Vivi: Make up my bed. I'll be there in 15.

Lilla: You're the best friend in the entire world.

Vivi: You're trying. I know it's hard.

I wait on the porch. When Vivi gets here, she sinks onto the stairs and puts her head on my shoulder. All of the joy that pulsed behind her texts is gone.

"What happened?"

"I didn't get picked for the museum," she says in a small voice.

"Oh, Vivi." I wrap my arms around her. "Why not?"

She rests her head on my shoulder. "She said I wasn't a good match for the children's museum. My crafts were too complicated, and I didn't seem to like little kids."

"Well…" I say. I want to support her, but Vivi doesn't like little kids. She calls them germ factories.

She laughs. "I know. They're the worst. Kate asked me what I'd do if a kid was sad and wanted to go home, and I said call their mom to come get them because we didn't need crying kids at camp."

I cover my mouth with my hands. I can't help it. "Vivi!"

"It just came out," she says, a little smile starting.

Sometimes keeping things to yourself is the right decision. It isn't the time to tell Vivi this though.

"What about the science camp?" The kids who go there are a little older, and Vivi's a science prodigy. She's perfect.

"Nope. She said they had some unusually strong applicants for science this year, and she'd call if there was an opening."

Uh-oh. I am the unusually strong applicant. One of them anyway. I never thought I would take Vivi's spot. Especially since I wanted the children's museum all along. I feel terrible. But also—even though it seems wrong—a little proud. Kate thought I'd be better at this than Vivi.

The only things I've ever been better at than Vivi are drawing and gymnastics, and I've always believed that's only because she never tried either one.

Before I can figure out what to say, my phone buzzes.

Knox: Guess what??? Children's museum! Colby too!!!

Even though I'm sad for Vivi, I smile at Knox's exclamation points.

"Figures," Vivi says, typing into her phone. "I guess you got art then?"

She's looking at her screen, so I don't have to answer. Which is good. It was only this afternoon she was upset with me, and I don't want to go back to that.

Vivi: What did you say when she asked what you'd do if a kid cried?

Knox: Build a fort with the giant blocks for him to hang out in until he felt better. I think I got extra points for assuming it was a boy.

Lilla: Giant fort was going to be your answer whatever the question, wasn't it?

Knox: Obvs. You guys are going to be so sad with your oil paints and your microscopes while Colby and I are living it up in the fake grocery store.

It's not the time, but I am, in fact, totally jealous.

Vivi: That's not how it's going down.

Knox: Why? Did they put Lilla in science too? That's awesome.

Vivi: No. They didn't pick me.

Seconds later, her phone rings. She goes over to the porch swing. A big part of me wants to follow her, so I can wrap my arm around her and so I can hear what they're saying. But she needs him more right now. And whatever giddy, girlie nonsense I felt this afternoon about Knox and his Suddenly Adorable Freckles, I am not getting weird about my two best friends talking on the phone.

When Vivi puts her phone away, she pats the swing. I join her, pulling my legs up under the big sweatshirt I put on after my shower. It's cooled down a lot since the afternoon.

"What did he say?"

"That I'm too brilliant to waste my time working with kids."

I know that Knox doesn't really think this. He'd love to be a teacher, but I'm glad he said it. I put my head on Vivi's shoulder. "He's right. And now you can do that coding camp. Where you will dominate."

"Yeah. And Colby offered to duel whoever took my place, but I said he didn't have to."

This would maybe be a good time to tell her who's taking her place, but I don't want to risk making her angry again.

"You know this doesn't have anything to do with how smart you are?"

"I guess. But it kind of makes me wonder…Do you still think I'll get into Grover?"

"Of course." Vivi's math scores were in the ninety-ninth percentile, which means literally no one did better than her, and she wrote an app last year that people actually downloaded from the Internet. It's perfect for the showcase.

"Hey," Vivi says. "I was so worked up about myself I forgot all about you. What's going on here?"

I take Vivi inside and we curl together on my bed while I whisper to her everything I heard Mom and Dad say.

Dad pokes his head in at one point, asking what we're up to.

I say, "Girl talk." This is mean because it makes him feel like I'd tell Mom if she were here, but I'm in kind of a mean mood. Let him feel left out for a change.

Vivi says that Dad is probably seeing someone, but says even though it's gross, it probably isn't serious if he doesn't want to tell me. My brain thinks she's right, but my stomach disagrees. I can barely even think the word—*stepmother*.

If I feel like a visitor here now, what will it be like when some unknown woman lives here? Or—*shudder*—if there are children? Stepsisters? Stepbrothers? Step-pets?

Vivi says I can move in with her if that happens. And that would be better than living with strangers, but still. I am an only child, and I am not made for sharing bathrooms. Also, I don't like when animals lick me. Though, now that I think about it, Vivi's sister also licks.

Neither of us can figure out what's up with Mom. Maybe it's another trip, but I don't know why that would be a secret. She goes off bug-hunting a couple of times a year. Vivi thinks she wants to travel more and Dad didn't want her to and that's why they got divorced and now she's afraid to tell me. But that doesn't make sense. He never seemed to mind when she was gone. (I guess that should have been my first clue.) And I never made it hard for Mom. I fall asleep wondering why she won't tell me what's going on.

In the morning, Vivi leaves at ridiculous early o'clock for soccer camp, and a little later, Dad goes to the museum. Instead of going up to see Mom, I play *Infinite Monkey Cage* podcasts, eat cereal out of the box, and work on my dream house.

Last year for my birthday, I got a kit to build a balsa-wood bungalow from my grandparents. It came with wood and a little lumber cutter and real architect's plans. It's taken ten months, but I've got it framed up, and I'm putting shingles on the roof. That's the last step before I get to do the inside.

In the beginning, I liked the challenge of reading the plans and cutting the wood just right and thinking about the way the colors on the walls would work together. But since the divorce, I've spent more time daydreaming. I can imagine living somewhere like this someday. A little two-bedroom home I get to decorate all by myself and fill with only the books and art and music I choose.

And when I'm working on the house, I can believe that someday I will have a life that can't be upended by anyone else's unhappiness.

CHAPTER 12

Fine

At noon, I head out to meet Vivi at her soccer camp. We're going to have lunch at her house before she reveals her next Summer of Brave challenge. I'm a little worried. It could be anything.

"I'll see you at the school tonight?" Mom asks when I go upstairs to say goodbye. "Vivi's parents are bringing you?"

Right. The magnet school meetings.

"Yeah, we'll meet you there," I answer.

She makes a sad face. "I feel like I never see you anymore."

Guilt hits me out of nowhere, setting off a little storm somewhere deep inside. It's not fair. Why should I feel guilty when she's the one keeping secrets?

"That's math for you," I say. "Divide my time in half, and it's going to be less."

I keep my voice light, but Mom sits back a little. "You remember I'm going to Chicago tomorrow?"

I didn't, but I nod. She said this to make me feel worse. And even though I know that, it still works. I can't let her leave while I feel like this, so I force a smile. "Do you have time to go out to breakfast first?"

Her eyes light up. "Sure, I'd like that."

"Me too." Sort of. Which I guess makes it one more lie, but that challenge is over anyway.

I take the long way to the middle school practice fields, walking along the river through campus so I can enjoy the quiet magic of the light in the trees. I take a few minutes to finish the sketch I started on the last day of school. It's a different time of day, but it works.

Walking this way—instead of through town—takes me to the boys' field first. And I know, however pretty the campus is, this is why I came the way I did. I want to watch Knox without Vivi watching me.

I meet Vivi and Knox after soccer all the time, but I always get Vivi first because sometime in the last couple years, being the only girl around a bunch of boys has gotten weird. I've never felt afraid. I'm just super aware that they're looking at me and seeing a *girl*, and I don't want to deal with it.

So I hang back near a cluster of trees where I'm out of the way. Even so, I find Knox easily in the middle of all the identically dressed boys. He plays differently than Vivi, who's all speed and focus. Knox laughs and trash-talks his friends and clowns with the ball. I've known him since I was four, and I've seen him play a million times. But I've never looked at him like this. And I can't help but wonder, why? Did some timer go off inside me, and Knox was in the line of fire?

If a crush is some stage I have to go through, it would be better with someone else. This is a friendship I want to keep.

Colby's out there. And Max, who I sat by during coding last year. And Aiden, who edged me out for first place in the science fair. I can totally see why someone might like any one of them. But looking at them doesn't give me that strange tingly warmth I felt crossing the creek yesterday. Maybe if one of them picked me up?

None of this makes sense.

"What are you doing here?" Vivi asks, coming up behind me. She must have got out early.

"I told you I'd meet you."

"But?" She looks back toward her field.

"I came through campus."

She looks out at Knox, who's finishing up. "Hmm."

Knox and Colby jog over. Knox slaps Vivi five and tugs my ponytail. I'm not sure how to rank these gestures. And I know it's wrong to try. But, really, do they mean something different? Is there some chart I could check on the Internet?

"What's the plan?" Knox asks.

"Home for lunch. Then walk over to the library," Vivi says, pleased with herself. "Lilla's going to check out a book."

"Why?" I ask.

"You're going to get a book you actually *want*," Vivi says. "On Monday."

Oh. I see where she's going with this. Mrs. Wilder works at the library on Mondays, and we have a history. "That's not nice," I say.

"Is someone going to tell me what's going on?" Colby asks.

"It's a stupid bet," Knox answers.

Vivi looks hurt. Probably I do too. I know Knox was only half kidding when he said he's glad his guy friends don't know what he does when he hangs out with us, but still. As frustrating as our Summer Wish can be, it's not a stupid bet. It's more.

Knox gives us both a look of apology but doesn't explain the wish to Colby. Instead he says, "Vivi's decided that Lilla and I need to be brave."

Colby looks puzzled. "What does that have to do with Mrs. Wilder?"

"Want to come find out?" Vivi asks.

"Wouldn't miss it," Colby says to Vivi. I guess I don't get a say.

"Library at two."

On the way to her house, I try to talk Vivi out of the plan. "How about if we go to the grocery store, and when the checkout girl asks how I am, instead of saying 'fine,' I'll tell her how I really am?"

"How are you really?"

I think about that for a minute. I'm worried about my parents, confused about Knox, a little nervous how things might be changing between me and Vivi, and freaked out about the whole magnet school thing, but I'm also thrilled about the summer camp. These are not exactly things I want to talk about though, especially with a grocery-store clerk.

"Fine, I guess."

"Mrs. Wilder it is then," Vivi says as she opens the door to the mudroom.

Then she leaps back, bumping into me. Looking over her shoulder, I see why. Her mom and dad are kissing. And not like parents. Like people in a movie. Her mom's sitting on the washing machine while her dad stands in front of her, his hands on her waist.

"Mom. Dad," Vivi says. "Get it together here."

Her mom leaps down from the washing machine. But she leans back against Vivi's dad while he wraps his arms around her, so I don't think she feels all that embarrassed.

"Hello, Lilla. Sorry about that."

"It's okay," I say. But tears well up in my eyes, and my chest feels heavy. Vivi doesn't want to see her parents acting like teenagers, but I'd give anything to see my parents together like this. Not only because my life would be better, but because it would feel like a promise of what it could be.

Some part of me believes the reason my parents got divorced is because Mom was too much for Dad, with her traveling and her big opinions and loud emotions. But Vivi's mom is a sociology professor, and she writes books and goes to conferences and argues with Vivi's dad using lots of words I don't understand, and he doesn't seem to mind at all. From what I just saw, I'd say he likes it. A lot.

Every time I come to Vivi's, I try to figure this out. Because my mom and dad argued too—in that way I thought was playful—but they got divorced. I can't understand the difference. And because of that, I don't know how to be. How difficult are you allowed to get before the people in your life want to leave?

"Sorry," Vivi's mom says again, and this time it means something different. She pulls me into a hug and strokes my hair. "I am very sorry, Lilla."

And then I'm sobbing in a way I never have in front of anyone—not my parents, not Vivi, not the therapist who kept telling me it was okay to cry in her office. Vivi's mom doesn't say anything but holds me. Vivi wraps her arms around both of us.

When I calm down, her mom puts her hands on my shoulders and pushes me back a little bit. "I know it's hard now. In some ways, it will always be hard, but it will get better too."

"How do you know?"

"Divorce isn't the only way things go wrong." When she says this, a flash of panic hits. Is someone in Vivi's family sick? But then I remember all the years between Vivi and Gabi and how sad Vivi's mom looked whenever she saw a baby during that time.

"Are you okay?" Vivi's mom asks.

I wipe my eyes. "I'm fine."

Vivi snorts.

CHAPTER 13

Kissing Books

"All right. What are the rules?"

We're in the courtyard in front of the library. Vivi, Knox, and Colby take turns sliding down the waxed stone arms on either side of the front steps. It's a beautiful old building, but I'm in no mood.

"Go tell Mrs. Wilder which book you want, Lilla," Knox says, laughter in his voice.

"And it has to be something you really want," Vivi says. "No pretending you suddenly can't wait to read *Black Beauty*."

"And no lying when she asks you questions," Knox adds.

"Including white lies," Vivi says.

"Why would you lie?" Colby asks. "I like talking to Mrs. Wilder about books."

"You wouldn't if you read the kind of books Lilla does," Vivi says.

Colby gives me look. "Okay. Now, I'm interested. Can we watch?"

"Of course," Vivi says just as I say, "Absolutely not."

"There's no way we're letting you go in there alone," Knox says.

"You think I'd lie to you?"

"Yes," all three of them say together.

"Fine." I fling open the door, and they scramble to follow me.

Mrs. Wilder was my third-grade teacher. When she retired, she started volunteering at the library on Mondays.

She likes to talk about the books you check out. This was great for a long time. We agreed that books about orphaned sets of twins were always better than books about dogs that die. We disagreed about Junie B. Jones, but liked arguing about it. I think Junie B. is hilarious. Mrs. Wilder wishes she wouldn't say "stupid" so much and that her mother yelled less. Mrs. Wilder also taught me to read graphic novels—I found all the pictures really distracting at first— and she introduced me to *Anne of Green Gables*, so I will always be grateful.

But.

Lately, I do not want to talk about the books I check out. They are just for me. I don't leave them lying around, because Mom finds my taste in books disappointing, and even Vivi gets one-word answers when she asks about them. Knox and Dad know better than to bring it up at all.

So I don't usually come to the library on Mondays. Because when Mrs. Wilder sees me in the young adult section, she starts saying things about swoony heroes and meet-cutes and all sorts of other words I do not want to hear out loud—especially from her—because talking about book boyfriends with grown-ups, even nice ones, is icky.

Vivi and Knox have been pushing me for a while to tell Mrs. Wilder that I want to be left alone about my books. But I can't make myself do it. It feels mean.

Almost right away, I find what I'm looking for—a book about a boy and a girl who fall for each other while leaving notes in a journal they hide all over the city. And bonus. The cover is all abstract reds and blues. No embarrassing close-ups of real kids kissing, which I could not have dealt with today with Knox smirking at me from across the library. I should have brought a bag to stuff the book in after I check it out.

When I go by the information desk, Mrs. Wilder says, "Hi, Lilla. What have you got?"

Vivi makes the I'm-watching-you sign with her fingers, while Knox mouths, "Yes, Lilla, what have you got?" His smile says he has a pretty good idea.

I turn my back to them and hold up my book to Mrs. Wilder.

"Oh, you'll like that," she says. "So cute and nothing inappropriate for younger readers."

Lately, this word comes up a lot around my reading. Inappropriate. But nothing I've read in the last year has been anywhere near as alarming as those feral cat books in the children's section that everyone kept pushing on me a while ago. They weren't my thing, but I know from Vivi that there were cats fighting and cats mating and a mother cat who put down her kid because he was some kind of evil cat villain or something. I can't imagine why anyone thinks that's more appropriate than two kids falling in love.

"If you like that one," Mrs. Wilder says, "you might like this too." She grabs a book from the return cart behind her. The cover has a boy and girl holding hands with hearts all over the place. I hop to put my body between the book and the audience behind me. Vivi giggles.

"I'm good. Thanks," I say quietly.

"Well, you'll have to tell me what you think of that one. I adored Dash."

Here is the moment. I look over my shoulder at Vivi. She gives me a thumbs-up. Colby's scrolling through his phone, but Knox smiles at me, encouraging now.

I don't want to hurt Mrs. Wilder's feelings or cause a scene. But I also don't want to have to do this whenever I come into the library. I can't figure out how much I should care about other people's feelings. How much of myself am I supposed to give up to make them happy?

Sensing something's wrong, Mrs. Wilder says, "Lilla? What is it?"

I hug my book to my chest, feeling my heart beat harder. This is such a small thing. In my head, I know that. But saying what I want out loud when it will make someone—especially a grown-up—unhappy feels huge.

But Vivi will be so disappointed if I give up. And Knox will win this round without even having to do his part of the challenge.

I take a deep breath. "I think I'm getting to a stage where I don't want to talk about my books so much?" My voice gets real quiet, but I say it. "They feel private?"

I can't tell if the charge that runs through me when I say this is fear or excitement.

"Oh!" Mrs. Wilder says, taking a step back. "Of course. I'm sorry."

I feel terrible. "No, I'm sorry," I say quickly. "It's not you. I don't want to talk about what I'm reading with anyone."

Mrs. Wilder touches my arm. She doesn't seem upset at all. "I understand," she says. "You're allowed to keep your reading a personal experience if that's what you want."

Is it really this easy? Can you just say what you want and people listen? I feel like I learned a magic trick.

Vivi squeezes me as soon as I get outside with my book. "You did it! And now you can go to the library without worrying about all that. It was worth it, wasn't it?"

"You do the best Summer Wishes," I admit.

Vivi grins. "So will you tell your parents about the magnet school now, instead of doing some supersecret Lilla plan?"

"I don't know." There's a big difference between telling Mrs. Wilder I'm growing out of talking about my books and telling my parents I'm a terrible daughter. Fortunately, Knox and Colby come out of the library then with their own books, so Vivi and I can stop talking about it.

Colby reaches around me to grab for my book. "I want to see what all the fuss was about."

Vivi slaps his hand.

"Hey!" he says.

Vivi looks at me.

"What?" I say.

"Tell Colby you don't want to talk about what you're reading."

Knox laughs. "I think your smackdown took care of that."

"Lilla needs to do it."

"Colby," I say. "I'd rather not talk about what I'm reading."

"That doesn't make me less curious," Colby says.

"Listen to Lilla," Vivi says. "She's still learning to speak up, and she needs the win."

"Celebrate at Cookie Mistake?" Knox asks.

"Can't," Colby responds. "I have to get home. Thanks for the entertainment, Lilla. Bye, Troublemaker." He tugs Vivi's ponytail.

"You're afraid if you stick around I'll make you improve yourself too."

"No danger of that," he says.

*

Once we're settled at a table in front of the bakery with cupcakes and drinks, I say, "What about Knox?"

"You're not done," Vivi says. "That program's tonight. It's time to tell your parents what you want for school. And what you don't want."

"Um, no. That's not how this works. Knox is next, or I win this round," I say. "Besides, maybe I'll hear something that will change my mind. I'm not totally sure what I want."

"What are you talking about?" Knox says. "Is this about whether you do drawing or science? Are your parents being pushy?"

Vivi looks at me and crosses her arms, letting me know it's time to talk. It's not that I want to keep this from Knox in particular. It's just the more I say it out loud, the more real it gets.

"Fine," I say to Vivi before looking at Knox. "I might not want to go to the magnet school at all."

Knox looks as shocked as Vivi did. I tell him all the things I told her.

"Wouldn't you miss us?" He looks hurt. Maybe this is a mistake.

"Of course. But I'd still see you both, right? You wouldn't stop being my friends because we didn't go to school together?"

"Never," he says, tossing his balled-up straw wrapper at me. "You're stuck with me."

I meet his eyes and smile.

Vivi clears her throat. "Me either."

I look down at my cupcake, equally embarrassed and happy.

"But then why go to that meeting tonight?" Knox asks.

"I told my mom and dad I'm still trying to decide between programs."

"Lilla, rip the band-aid off," Vivi says.

I shake my head. "Not yet. I might still go. They really want this for me. And they're my parents. I can't say I want to give up this amazing experience because I'd rather do color guard than homework. They'll never understand."

"Color guard?" Knox asks.

"I think it would be fun to twirl a flag and march in parades. And I like those little white boots they wear."

Confused, Knox and Vivi study me. Vivi opens her mouth, closes it, and opens it again.

"Never mind," I say. "That part's not important. Let's talk about what's next for Knox."

Vivi smiles. "I've got a good one for him, but he has to wait till Saturday."

"What?" he says. "Why?" He's nervous. Good.

"You're going to go to No Strings Attached and tell Jax what you're playing for the showcase."

"You are not a nice girl, Vivian," Knox says. No Strings Attached is the hipster music store where Knox likes to hang out. Jax is a college student who works weekends, plays the guitar, and wears one of those knitted hats even in the summer. He talks about bands Knox has never heard of, but Knox always pretends he has, and Knox always acts annoyed when Jax calls him "Little X." But I know he wants to be Jax when he grows up.

Knox keeps his feelings about bubblegum pop a secret from Jax, and this must be what he plans to play next week. Vivi's a genius. This is a perfect Knox task to go with my trip to the library.

I open my mouth to ask what he's playing so I can see exactly how embarrassing this is going to be, but Knox shakes his head before I get words out. "I don't have to tell Lilla, right? I can surprise her?"

I'm a little disappointed, but I like that he wants to surprise me.

Vivi nods. "Surprises are okay."

Knox meets my eyes and some of that feeling from the creek sparks.

Being brave isn't all bad.

CHAPTER 14

Well Rounded

That night I bounce my legs up and down while I sit on a hard metal folding chair between Vivi and Mom.

Mom didn't freak out when I said I wanted to stay after and go to the arts session with Dad, but she got quiet. The way she does when she is Disappointed in Me. Even though she didn't say anything this time, I could hear all her words from before. About how women have worked so hard to open up opportunities in math and science. And how all I have to do is walk through the door. And how my generation is so lucky.

I feel sick.

Mom didn't like when I quit gymnastics, but she gave in pretty easy. Gymnastics wasn't a career or even something I'd do in college, and it wasn't like I was breaking any barriers doing it.

But this. This is different. It's clear Mom would not be thrilled if I said I wanted to do the arts program. She'd hate that I'd be giving up my chance to be a Girl in Science.

Still, I know that if told her I really love drawing, she would support me. In time, she'd get it. But there is literally no way I can tell her—or Dad—that I don't want to do either one.

I'm not sure how to explain it. I'm not lazy. I just don't want to give up everything so I can be good at one thing. And I don't want to keep taking classes with girls who cry when they get B's and boys who argue their way into A's. And when I grow up, I don't want to spend my entire life doing one thing. Like my parents.

I'm relieved when the woman at the podium—some kind of principal, I'd guess, from her gray suit—starts on time. I want to get this over with. She goes over the admissions requirements—test scores, grades, showcase exhibit.

Some parts do sound pretty cool. There's a research class where you get to work with a scientist at the college. And a few sports. For girls—soccer, softball, field hockey, and track, which sound an awful lot like Prisha's list of appropriate girl sports.

When it's time for questions, only grown-ups speak. They ask about the admission process and college placement and test scores. The average SAT score for Grover Academy students is 150 points higher than for kids at Morningside.

"This is why this is so important," Mom whispers. "It's going to launch your whole life."

Then one woman—I'm not sure whose mom she is—says, "What about the arts?"

I sit up in my chair.

The woman at the podium says everyone needs to take half a credit in fine or performing arts. Half a credit. You could round it to zero.

Both Mom and Vivi turn to me because they know I care about this. I smile like this is totally fine.

It is not totally fine. Going here would mean giving up half of myself.

"Do students in the science track have opportunities to take classes on the arts side?" the mom asks. "I'd like Ian to be well rounded."

"This is a school for *gifted* kids," the woman at the podium responds. "Why would you want your child to spend his time on something he'll only ever be mediocre at? It takes ten thousand hours to become expert. The kids we admit—to both tracks—have enormous potential, but they need to commit. For well rounded, I'd suggest Morningside."

There's some nervous laughter. Mom nods enthusiastically, and the queasiness in my stomach kicks into overdrive.

I don't hear the last few questions. I sort of can't believe that I'm not even thirteen years old and everyone seems to think it's perfectly right and good that I make a decision about the Rest of My Life.

Mom squeezes my hand. "It sounds great, doesn't it?" I

nod and look at Vivi. She pushes her lips together in sympathy, and my tears well up. I need a minute to get myself together before I have to do this again with Dad.

"I have to go to the bathroom," I say.

Hearing the tremor in my voice, Mom looks closely. "Are you okay?"

"Sure. Allergies. I'll just…" I wave toward the side door. "And then meet Dad out front."

Mom squeezes me. "Love you."

"You too." I leap out of my seat.

I'm already in the hall by the time I see that Vivi followed me. I turn away. I can't deal with her telling me to speak up right now.

Then my phone buzzes.

Dad: Where are you? It's about to start.

Lilla: Bathroom. Just a minute.

Dad: Oh! Sorry.

Dad's freaked out by cell phone use in bathrooms. It's useful sometimes.

"It'll be okay," Vivi says. "Whatever you choose, your parents will come around. Eventually."

"I'm just not this kind of kid. But I don't know how to tell them."

She pulls me into a hug. "You'll figure it out." This is why I love Vivi. She pushes me, but she listens too.

When I don't move for what is definitely too long, Vivi

says, "Come on. We'd better find your dad."

He's standing in the lobby in front of the auditorium, looking at his phone.

"What took you so long?" he says. His face gets all nervous. "Did something happen in the bathroom?"

"No. What would happen in the bathroom?"

"You know," he whispers. "Secret things."

I swear Dad's biggest regret about the divorce is that he might someday have to talk to me about my period. This is probably why he's out looking for someone to be my stepmother.

"Gah. No. Just." I stop talking because I'm distracted by Knox, who is scowling up at his dad as they walk through the lobby. I'm surprised. School events are usually his mom's thing. Knox shakes his head and storms off into auditorium. His dad follows. He does not look happy.

"Let's go inside," I say to Dad.

Vivi hugs me. "Good luck."

"Are you meeting us after?"

"I don't think so." She holds up her phone. "There's some pickup soccer going on outside. I'm going to ask if I can do that instead of going home right away."

"Okay. I'll text when I get home."

Dad and I find a seat. Searching, I see the back of Knox's head up near the front. He's sitting ramrod straight, as far from his dad as he can get in his chair.

A woman takes the podium. Instead of a suit, she's wearing a flowing orange skirt. A bright pink scarf holds back her mountain of curls. They lean pretty hard into this arts-science divide.

"That's Marian Ortega," Dad says. "She's a painter and one of the associate principals."

I pull out my phone.

Lilla: You okay?

Knox: Not now. It's about to start.

"Shouldn't you pay attention?" Dad says. He means *pay attention!*

"Apparently."

I don't listen as closely this time. Partly because I just heard all the bits about how the school works and the sports and the clubs and partly because I'm worried about Knox. He doesn't get upset easily.

I do catch that you get to take an art class at the college your senior year and do a public exhibition in the city, but that you only get into AP physics or chemistry if there's room after the science kids sign up.

"But noooooo!" someone calls out, and everyone laughs.

No one asks about being well rounded.

"Very exciting," Dad says once we're in the lobby. I'm watching the exit for Knox. Dad gives me a little squeeze. "I'm so proud of you. I would have killed the family dog for a chance like this."

Yikes. No strong feelings there.

"Thanks," I say, not looking at Dad. "You can go home if you want. I'm going to do ice cream with Knox." I gesture toward where Knox and his dad are coming out of the auditorium, a good three feet of space between them.

"And Vivi? She'll be there too?" Dad says. There's something more than curiosity in his voice. Maybe suspicion? His eyes move back and forth between Knox and me. Is he worried about us being alone together? Because Knox is a boy?

"Vivi's outside," I say. Another white lie. I never noticed how often I did this until Vivi asked me to keep track.

"Okay," Dad says. "Have fun then." The relief on his face tells me I'm right, and that makes me a little angry because whatever this new thing is that I'm feeling, Knox is also the boy I went to kindergarten with.

I want to tell Dad to stop being ridiculous, but I'm afraid that if I do, I will give myself away because everything is so complicated now. Knox is my friend, but he is also all of a sudden this Cute Boy Person. If I say too much, Dad might see how I feel and not let me go with him.

I can't let that happen. Because whatever else is going on, Knox is sad tonight, and he needs someone to talk to, and I am his friend.

And that will always be true.

I hope.

CHAPTER 15

Bad Boys

I catch up to Knox and his dad out in front of the school. Out loud, I say, "You still up for ice cream?" My eyes ask if he's okay. Knox gives me the smallest of headshakes.

His dad smiles. Really big. I take a step back. "Hi, Lilla. Good to see you. Maybe you can coax a few words out of my son."

"Hi, Mr. Donohue," I say quietly, trying to figure out what Knox wants me to do. "Is it okay if Knox comes out with Vivi and me for a bit?"

"Sure!" he says in a loud voice. He claps Knox on the shoulder, but Knox jerks away. "You're a lucky guy. Going out with two pretty girls."

"Pretty isn't the most important thing about them," says Knox. "They're, like, actual human beings."

Uh-oh. I have no idea what's going on here. Knox and his dad have never gotten along super great, but usually he's more silent than snarky.

"I'll let your mother know where you are."

"I have a phone," says Knox. "Don't bother."

"See you this weekend then."

"Yeah. Those are the rules."

His dad leaves.

Knox watches him go, takes a deep breath, and looks at his shoes. "I don't actually feel like ice cream tonight. Why don't you and Vivi go?"

"Knox," I say quietly. "What's going on?"

He shakes his head a little. There are tears in the corners of his eyes. This is terrifying. I haven't seen Knox cry since second grade when he fell off a slide and broke his arm. He wipes his eyes with the back of his hands.

"Sorry," he says.

"Let's get out of here." I pull him forward.

"What about Vivi? I don't think..." His voice trails off. This must be about the divorce. That's the one thing he never talks about with her.

"She's playing soccer," I say. "She's not expecting us."

He stuffs his hands in his pockets. "Okay."

It's twilight, and the air has that kind of coolness that only happens on summer evenings. Without talking, Knox and I head toward the river.

Near the college library, there's a ledge of wide, flat rocks that you can only find by pushing through a thicket of bushes. Our spot since we were little. Sometimes we find an old soda can or initials scratched into the stone, so I know other people come here. But I'm always surprised when I see that stuff. It feels like ours alone.

Tonight, we kick off our shoes and sit on the edge. Knox's feet reach the water, but I can only touch if I point my toes.

I really want to know what's going on, but I leave it be. Knox wouldn't have cried unless it was big, and he's probably rattled having done it in front of me. He'll talk when he's ready.

A dragonfly floats down, touches the water, and rises back up. Anisoptera. Mom says girl dragonflies sometimes pretend to be dead so the boy dragonflies leave them alone.

I get it, but it seems extreme.

"My dad's getting remarried," Knox says finally.

Oh. The tears make sense now. I would have felt sorry for him before, but now that I've been thinking about how awful it would be if Dad remarried, I'm even more sympathetic. "To who?" I ask.

He gives me a look. "Ashley. She graduates from college this year." There is so much he's not saying packed into those words. But I've been around for all of it, so I know.

When we were in fourth grade, Knox had this really great babysitter. But she broke her leg toward the end of the year, and her best friend, Ashley, took over. Knox's parents divorced three months later.

I can't imagine how awful this must be. Knowing the person who ended your parents' marriage is going to be in your life forever. Or at least until your dad moves on again.

"I'm sorry." I lean in to him. Before, I might have taken his hand or even put my arm around him, but after the creek, that all feels like too much.

"He was all proud. Said, 'She's closer to your age than mine!'"

"Yuck."

"I won't tell you what he said next, but it was even worse. He's awful. I can't figure out if he was always like this or if it's new."

I'm about to ask if it matters, but then I remember crying in Vivi's kitchen, and the way I keep trying to figure out what Mom and Dad's choices mean for me. Knox has to be doing the same thing. Maybe he's worried that if this is who his dad always was, then it's inside him too.

"You're different than he is," I say.

Knox turns his head to look at me but doesn't speak, and I'm suddenly aware of how close his face is to mine. My heart beat speeds up a little.

"You are."

"This sucks in so many ways," he says. "But you want to know the worst?"

I nod.

"The way he told me like I was one of the guys—not his son. Like he doesn't want to be a father."

I hadn't planned on talking about this with Knox, but being honest feels like one of the only things I can do for him. We talked a lot about the divorces back when they happened, but we haven't for a while. Now that I think about it, it's been a long time since we've been together without Vivi or Colby. As terrible as this news is, it's sort of nice to do it again.

"My dad isn't like yours," I say.

"I know," he says quickly.

"But he's seeing someone. He doesn't want to tell me who."

"Oh. Sorry."

"Yeah. And my mom's keeping a secret. A big one, I think. But I don't know what."

"It's worse when they don't tell you what's going on. I guess I should thank my dad for that much."

Knox is right. The most horrible part of the divorce was the two weeks before they told me. I could tell something terrible was happening, but I didn't know what. Whatever is going on with them now feels a little bit like that. Like I'm alone in the dark.

"It's weird," I say. "Until my parents got divorced, I didn't realize how much of their lives have nothing to do with me."

Knox makes a sound that is almost, but not quite, a laugh. "With my parents, I've always been pretty clear about that."

"I know," I say. I want to take his hand, but I'm not brave enough. "The thing is, it might be true of all parents, even the ones who stay together?"

"What do you mean?"

"I was at Vivi's the other day and her parents..." My voice trails off. I cannot say they were kissing. Out loud. To Knox.

"What?" he says, looking mystified.

"They were just really happy. And I've been thinking about it, and I don't think they stay together because of Vivi and Gabi. They like each other. That's why they stay married. When you're little, you think you're the center of your parents' whole world. But maybe you're not?"

I look at Knox to see if any of this makes sense. After a little bit, he says, "That shouldn't make me feel better. But it does."

It might make me feel better too. If I'm not the only thing that matters in my parents' world, then maybe I don't have to make them happy. Maybe that's their job.

"Ice cream?" Knox stands, obviously wanting to put all this behind us for a little while.

While I check my phone, I admit to myself that I'm a little disappointed. I'm a big fan of ice cream, but I already miss the warmth of his shoulder next to mine. "I only have half an hour."

"We can eat while I walk you home."

"Sounds good." I get to my feet. "You're going to be okay?"

"Yeah." He gives me a quick hug, stepping back before I can settle on whether I'm excited or embarrassed or nervous. "Thanks, Lil."

My heart thumps. "No problem."

＊

Mom and I get up early to hit our favorite pancake place before she goes off to Chicago, and I head to my first day of training at the museum. She orders scrambled eggs, whole-wheat toast, and a half a grapefruit. She's healthy like that. I order sticky toffee pancakes. Because to do anything else would be wrong.

We both focus on our phones until the food comes, but once we're eating, she says, "Nervous about today?"

I shake my head. All the hard stuff is over. The only thing I have left to be nervous about is Vivi finding out that I got her science spot. And I'm going to tell her. Soon.

"What about you?" I ask. "What is this talk? You don't usually have conferences in June."

"This is something a little different."

I look up from my pancakes when she doesn't go on. There's something in her voice. Nervousness? Excitement? Could she be seeing someone too? Is the talk an excuse for a weekend away?

When I was little, Mom and I spent every day together all summer long, unless I was at one of the museum camps. Dad still had to work at the museum every day, but she took summers off. We'd go to the lake or read in her home office or drive all over looking for the best ice cream. We had no secrets. She knew all about my friends and my teachers and my books, and she talked about things I didn't really understand yet—rivalries at work and how wasps communicate.

But now it's different. I can tell she doesn't want to hurt me. And I don't want to make her angry. And so we're quiet. And confused.

"I'm sharing my research with some colleagues at Northwestern. And I'm a little nervous. They're pretty smart."

I smile. "You'll do great."

She looks out the window for a while and then says, "Can I ask you something?"

"Anything," I say, thinking I might find out what the heck is going on.

"I was on the phone with Vivi's mom the other day, and she said you went to the library?"

"Yes?" I say. I'm at the library twice a week in the summer. This is not news.

"I wanted to ask who you were with."

"Vivi and Knox?" This is like asking if I was wearing shoes. Who else would I be with?

"No one else? No other boys?"

"Colby," I say. "Knox's friend." My cheeks get hot, and noticing this—and realizing what it's going to make Mom think—only makes it worse.

"So," she says with a little grin. "Tell me about Colby. Vivi's mom says he's a bit of a troublemaker. Your father and I were pretty surprised. I don't think either one of us thought the bad boy thing would draw you in."

"Mom, can you not?" I am completely horrified. And I don't know what to go after first. That Vivi's mom talked to my parents about boys. That Mom and Dad were talking about who I like. That they think it's Colby. Or that Colby—honor roll, band geek, soccer-playing Colby—is a bad boy. Whatever that means. Not that he wouldn't be thrilled to hear it.

"Colby's not…I mean, I'm not…Why are we even talking about this?"

"I always had a bit of a thing for the bad boys myself," the waitress says, refilling Mom's coffee cup. Surprised, Mom and I look up at her. "Just saying," she adds before she goes.

I put my face in my hands and say, "Please tell me it's time for you to go. Or me to go. Or for time to stop all together. Any one of those would be fine, really."

"Not quite," Mom says with a smile. "Is there anything going on you'd like to talk about? Maybe not Colby, but someone else?"

Something in her voice makes me think she has a particular someone else in mind. And probably the right one this time.

Slowly, I raise my head from my hands. And I think about Knox and Vivi and Dad and bird-nesting and Mom's secret and high school. But I don't know where to begin. Vivi would say start with what's easy. But I don't think any of this qualifies.

So I shake my head. "No. I'm fine."

CHAPTER 16

Team Building

Prisha jumps up and down, clapping her hands. "Go, go, go!"

I'm balancing an egg on a spoon, weaving through an obstacle course across the floor of the children's museum.

If you drop the egg, you have to clean it up with only one napkin. A few minutes ago, Colby and Knox had to use their bare hands to get all of their splattered egg. This is not something I ever want to do. First, I don't love how raw eggs feel. Honestly, if I think about eggs too much, I can't eat them at all. And second, I do not want that kind of attention. So I am going slowly. Much to the frustration of Drew, my teammate. When we met, the first thing he told me was his IQ score. The second thing was that he had to be homeschooled because he was two grade levels ahead.

He seemed to expect that I would faint from the shock of

it all and not that I would say, "I didn't know homeschooled kids did science."

He'd raised an eyebrow. "And I didn't know public school kids went to museums."

We are not friends.

So far, we've built towers out of toothpicks and marshmallows, held hands while sliding a hula-hoop around the circle, and learned the camp chants. Drew gave me Helpful Advice during each activity. I would like to thank him by pressing this egg into his chest, but there is the drawback of egg goo, and besides, my careful pace seems to be bothering him plenty.

"You could try," Drew says when I hand the spoon to him. I can't believe Kate picked him instead of Vivi. What was she thinking?

"Lean in, Lilla!" Matt shouts. I don't know what that means. But even if I did, I don't think I'd take advice from someone wearing a backward baseball cap and flip-flops. Matt is one of the college students Kate picked to be an associate director, so, along with the other associate director, Molly, he's mostly in charge.

He is one of those boys—men, maybe, I'm not sure how I'm supposed to think about college students—who is always doing loud claps and bumping fists and telling girls to smile. This morning he said "my fraternity" forty-six times while talking during breaks. His other favorite words are *shade*, *totes*, and *psyched*.

After Molly explained the egg game this morning, he patted her on the head. I can tell *she's* a grown-up because she didn't stab him with her spoon.

For reasons I don't understand, Knox seems to like Matt. He mirrors Matt's posture the same way he does with Jax at the music store. Only with Jax, Knox goes all slouchy. Being around Matt makes Knox stand straight up and throw back his shoulders. Like a doorman.

When the race is over, we get a ten-minute break.

The high-school kids, who are the senior counselors, throw themselves into the beanbag chairs in the reading corner.

Prisha skips over to me. "Do you want to come home with me after?"

"I don't know." I'm not sure what Vivi's doing, and it feels weird to make plans without her. Especially since I know she'd love to be here with us. Or with me at least. But I also don't know how to say this to Prisha without making it seem like I'm asking Vivi's permission. Which I'm not doing. I care about Vivi. That's all. "My mom's out of town, and my dad might want me home."

"Just ask."

I pull out my phone. Prisha's looking over my shoulder, so I have to tell her the truth. "I want to check with Vivi too. She'll expect to hear from me." Vivi would think it was pretty weird if I didn't text her to check in after camp. Especially if she found out later that I'd been with Prisha.

"Oh," Prisha says, sounding hurt.

"It's just…It's hard for her. She really wanted to be here."

"Forget it then." Prisha gives a little smile.

"I'm sorry. I definitely want to do something sometime. But there's a lot going on right now. And I'm spending all day here with you." Which Vivi is jealous about. I mean, I would be too.

"Sure. No big thing," Prisha says, but I can tell she doesn't mean it.

I don't know why it has to be like this. I wish Vivi and Prisha could like each other. Or at least believe that I like them both.

When Matt returns, he claps his hands again, making me jump. "Let's circle up!"

Kate joins us. "Tomorrow, we'll move into our museum groups, but I want us to finish today with each of you sharing why you applied to be a counselor."

Some of the answers are serious. A high-school girl says she wants to figure out if she should be a teacher. Others are silly. Aman, one of the senior science counselors, says he wants to spend time in the free air-conditioning.

Colby says, "I knew it was the only way I'd get my hands on that giant catapult. I have so many plans." So maybe he is a little bit of a troublemaker.

Knox leans across two people to fist-bump Colby, but when it's his turn to share, he's sincere. "I just want to be somewhere happy a couple hours a week."

Tears fill my eyes. Knox is always nothing but joy. But

his life at home has probably been a mess since his dad's announcement.

I wish I could protect him from all of it. Because even if you're not the center of your parents' world, everything they do gets to you somehow. The best you can do is lock it away for a little while.

Thinking about this makes me change the answer I planned to give—that I wanted to help girls find a place for themselves in science. I'm a little embarrassed about being honest about my feelings with a room full of strangers, so my voice is quiet when I say, "I wanted something that was mine."

"Big-girl voice, Lilla," Kate says. "This place is going to be full of kids next week. They need to hear you."

Drew laughs.

It's strange. I never felt like this in gymnastics meets, even though so many more people were watching. But I hate talking in front of groups of people.

Everyone is waiting, though, so I try again, a little louder this time. "I wanted to do something because I enjoyed it, not because it would impress people."

Afterward, Kate dismisses us. Matt comes over and squeezes my shoulder. "You don't have to be shy, Lilla. We're all friends here."

I want to tell him to keep his hands off me and that being quiet is not the same as being shy, but I know he doesn't mean anything, so I say, "Thanks," and step away.

Knox and Matt do fist bumps with fireworks, and Matt leaves.

"You want to come over tonight?" Knox asks. "Mom's feeling sorry for me because of the Ashley thing, so she said she'd order pizza. Video games? Movies? Whatever you want."

I guess this just-the-two-of-us thing from last night wasn't a fluke. I'm wondering if I'll have time to wash my hair when Knox's brown eyes go serious. "Thanks for yesterday," he says. "I can't talk to anyone else about that stuff."

His look sets everything inside me whirring. Like the time Vivi made us coffee milkshakes before bed and forgot to use decaf.

Colby lands beside us with a leap. "Can she come?"

I look at Colby.

"I already texted Vivi," Knox says. "She can come if you do."

He already texted Vivi. First. He texted her first. What does that mean? And Colby's coming. So this is a friend thing.

"Well?" Knox says.

"I'll ask my dad when I get home."

"'Kay," he says, totally relaxed. "We can go old-school if you want. Monopoly? Clue?"

"Exploding Kittens?" I ask.

"You name it." Knox links his pinkie with mine and gives my hand a little shake. "I owe you."

I am so confused.

CHAPTER 17

Different Now

At home, I freak out about what to wear. Because I want to look pretty. And okay, if you want to get right down to it, it's not just that I want to look pretty.

I want to look pretty for Knox. There. Not so scary to admit. At least to myself.

I pull on a green polka-dot sundress. It's super cute, but too fancy for playing games with friends, and Dad was already edgy about letting me go over there at night. Who knows what he's thinking after how weird he was about Knox last night and that talk I had with Mom about Colby this morning. The thing about having Committed Co-Parents is they still seem to spend a whole lot of time sharing news about me.

I change into black capri leggings and this floaty navy top

my mom got me on a trip of hers. I've never worn it before. Wide straps curve over the shoulders, and the top is tight across my chest, but the rest billows out around me.

It's good. I like the shape of me in it. When I was doing gymnastics, I was all straight lines and muscles. But I'm softer now. I gained ten pounds when I stopped going to the gym every day. I know from locker-room conversations and magazines I'm supposed to be all sad about this, but I'm not. I like it.

I put my hair up into a high ponytail like Prisha's and put on just a tiny bit of makeup. I usually don't wear any because Vivi always notices and makes fun of me, but I don't think it's so wrong that I like the way I look with a little lip gloss and mascara.

When I go into the kitchen to say goodbye, Dad looks up from the skillet, and his eyes widen. "You look nice," he says. "Grown up."

"Is that okay?" I say. Maybe it's too much?

"Yeah. Just unexpected. Lots of changes this year." I can't tell what he's feeling about this.

He turns the flame down on the burner and faces me, still holding the spatula. "Knox's mom said you're going to eat there? With Vivi...and this Colby."

"We're having pizza," I say, waiting for the real question. Which had better not be about Colby.

He looks at the ground. "Things are pretty rough for Knox right now, huh?"

Oh. Thank goodness this is what he wants to talk about. Not me and boys and growing up.

"She told you about Mr. Donohue?" I ask.

"Yeah...and..." He looks at the ground again, and my relief turns into worry. Is he going to use this as an excuse to tell me about who he's seeing? I want him to be honest. I do. But I'm not sure I'm ready to talk about this.

My parents always juggled their schedules so one of them was home with me. I haven't had a babysitter since I was tiny, so I don't have to worry about that. But what if it's a teacher? That would be awful. My brain runs through a slideshow of all the women who teach at the middle school. None seem likely. That assistant principal from the magnet school? That one he said was an artist. How did he know that?

"What, Dad?" I say.

"I want you to know I'll be careful about who I bring into your life. You can trust me."

"Okay." Easy to say. But when you've put me through a divorce and are dating No One Serious in secret, trust is a pretty big thing to ask. "Anything else?"

"That's all."

"Okay," I say again, trying not to let my sadness leak into my words.

Outside, the light's bright enough that it sends me back in for my sunglasses. After going through both my rooms, I find them in Mom's kitchen.

The sunglasses hunt makes me late, but I don't want to take my bike, 'cause Dad's picking me up. The last time he put it in the trunk, the chain got all messed up, and neither of my parents are great with repairs. To make up time, I head up one of the busy border streets between the college and the city instead of going through campus.

This route takes me right by an ice-cream shop where I have a gift card Mom got from a student and passed on to me. I pull out my phone to ask Vivi what I should get, but before I finish typing, there's a whistle.

A loud one.

And not a singing-a-song whistle. Or a calling-a-taxi one. But one of those whistles that men do in cartoons to women who walk by construction sites. I didn't know this happened in real life.

I look across the busy street to see what's going on. But there's no one.

"Over here," a guy's voice says.

Slowly, I turn toward the building I'm standing in front of. A fraternity. Two guys—college students—are sitting on the front porch.

The whistle must have come from them. A spike of fear nearly swamps me. I take a deep breath, trying to steady myself.

"Oh," one says with a laugh. "Sorry. Catch you in a few years, sweetheart."

I shake my head, backing away. A nervous laugh escapes.

"'Kay," I say.

Then it gets worse. Because then one of the guys says, "Lilla?" The amusement on his face turns into horror.

Matt. From the museum. I didn't recognize him without his hat and with sunglasses. He stands and takes a step toward me. His movement brings me back into my senses. I don't want him any closer, but I also don't want to make a scene, so I dart into the street, trying to put some kind of barrier between us.

A car lays into its horn, making me jump a good foot into the air. Matt shouts something behind me, but I don't turn back. Another car screeches to a stop. I run in front of it toward the campus. Someone yells behind me. I can't tell if it's Matt or the driver, and I don't stay to find out.

For the first time, the campus doesn't feel safe. But I've walked this path between my new neighborhood and my old one hundreds of times. I don't need to think to go forward.

"Lilla, wait up!" a familiar voice calls.

I don't know why, but I turn and fold my hands over my chest. A completely useless act of protection. I want to be covered.

"Hey," Colby says as he catches up.

Colby is safe. I don't need to be afraid, but my body will not listen. My heart pounds, and I shiver. My hands are so cold.

"Are you okay?"

I open my mouth to speak, ready to reassure him, but words won't come out.

"You're crying. What happened?" His voice has a strange intensity. Something about the way he says this makes me realize how much worse this could have been. What happened was so small compared to what could have happened.

But it doesn't feel small.

"You're shivering." Colby pulls off his backpack and hands me a sweatshirt. "Put that on."

I stuff my arms in and zip it up. Grateful. With my skin covered and Colby next to me, I feel safe for the first time since I heard that whistle.

"I might need to sit down for a minute," I say, moving toward a bench. My knees feel weak.

Colby sits, leaving a foot of space between us. I'm glad. I don't want anyone to touch me. I put my head between my legs, letting the dizziness fade.

"I was on my way to Knox's when I saw you. I'm going to tell them we're late."

I can't go over there tonight and pretend everything is normal. To try to figure out what's going on with Knox and me. The thought makes me sick to my stomach. I don't want to think about that stuff anymore. Maybe ever again. And I need time to make sense of this in my own head before I talk about it with anyone else. Even Knox and Vivi. And I definitely can't talk about it with Colby there.

"Can you tell them I don't feel well? That I'll see them tomorrow?"

Colby gives me a long look, not sure what to think, but starts typing.

My own phone buzzes. Even though they won't be able to see me, I feel like I need to get myself together before I pick it up. I wipe my eyes and then my nose with the cuffs of Colby's sweatshirt.

Then I fold back the sleeves to hide the evidence. Lady-like. Colby winces, but doesn't say anything. He's a trouper. Knox and Vivi text me at the same time on different threads.

Vivi: What's wrong?

Lilla: Some stomach thing. I don't think I should come over to-night. I don't want to make you two sick.

Vivi: Poor baby. I could bring you chicken soup.

Lilla: Maybe tomorrow. If I don't feel better.

I switch over to Knox.

Knox: Colby said you're sick?

Lilla: Yeah. Sorry.

Knox: Not your fault. Will you be at the museum tomorrow?

Lilla: I hope so. I'm going to bed early.

Knox: Feel better.

Colby offers to walk me home. I don't argue.

We're quiet as we walk. I don't know Colby well enough to talk about what happened. And I can't talk about this to Knox. He likes Matt, and even if he didn't, how could he understand how that whistle made me feel? I wouldn't have understood myself until it happened. And Vivi?

Vivi who wants me to be brave. She'd be so disappointed. I laughed and said "'kay"? Who does that? I wish I had shouted or slapped him or even called for help. I wish I were the kind of person who fights back.

At my house, Colby says, "Are you going to be okay?"

"Sure. Thanks for coming with."

"I have sisters." Colby may not know exactly what happened, but he has some idea. For some reason, this brings tears to my eyes again.

I unzip his sweatshirt to give it back, but he shakes his head. A little frantically.

I manage a laugh. "Sorry. I'll wash it first."

"Take care." He touches my arm in a completely normal way, but I have to force myself not to pull back.

Everything is different now.

CHAPTER 18

Aftermath

When I open the door, Dad calls, "Lilla?"

"Yes." My voice comes out surprisingly normal.

Instead of answering, he mumbles something. As I come toward the kitchen, I see he's on the phone. Maybe Mom?

But he says, "No, she's back. I'm sorry. I don't think this is going to happen tonight. Duty calls. I know. Me too. Bye."

Oh.

Not Mom.

This is actually happening. Dad steps out of the kitchen, wiping his hands on a towel.

"Who was that?" I ask.

"On the phone?" he says. "No one. A friend. Someone from work."

"Is this a guessing game?" I can't believe he's standing

here, looking me in my eyes, and lying. I guess this is not my night to be treated like someone who matters.

"Are you okay? Did you and Vivi have a fight? Whose sweatshirt is that?"

I answer the easiest question. "Colby's."

"Oh." He's quiet a moment. "Did you and Knox have a fight? About this Colby?" I don't even want to know what story he's building there. I don't have the energy for it. Especially since he is obviously not interested in sharing the details of his life with me.

I want my mom. I want to lie down on the bed and have her rub my back and tell me it's going to be okay. But she's in Chicago doing I don't know what, and I'm here with Dad, who is not great at showing emotion and lies and seems a little afraid of me right now. Because I'm about to cry. Or am crying, I guess. It's not the sobbing kind, but the one where tears keep leaking out.

"I don't feel well. I'm going upstairs to lie down. I'll sleep up there tonight." My softest blanket is up there. And *Anne of Green Gables*. I need a comfort book. And to be left alone.

"Lilla, I don't..." Dad says.

"What?"

"I'm not sure you should be up there. Without your mom. It's her space, and she and I didn't think to talk about this."

"It's my house too." My voice breaks. I can't believe he's making even this little thing so hard. "My room is up there."

"You have a room here. That's why we did it like this."

I shake my head. "Giving me two rooms didn't fix anything. You and Mom destroyed my family. You don't get bonus points for making the aftermath easier for you." My voice is soft, but Dad acts as if I shouted.

"Calm down. Whatever's going on, all this drama isn't going to make it better. Your family hasn't been destroyed. It's just different."

"Sure. I know." I need to get away before everything I've been thinking the last year flies out of my mouth.

He blinks. "I'll text your mom. Let her know you're sleeping upstairs."

"Thanks." I stop in my downstairs room to grab my speaker and the handbook Kate asked us to study tonight. The strange thing is even though I just told Dad how terrible the divorce has been for me, I feel like I suddenly understand Mom's decision to end things. I'll bet she felt alone with feelings a lot.

Like I am tonight.

Upstairs, I turn on every light, put on the slow, sad music Vivi hates, and stare into my closet. I have to figure out what to wear tomorrow.

I have a feminist mother. And I took health from a teacher who liked to Get. Into. It. I know—in my head—that what happened wasn't my fault. That what I wear doesn't give anyone permission to touch me or whistle at me.

But.

Tonight was the first time I ever dressed for a boy. And look what happened. It feels like I brought this on myself.

Maybe Kate was onto something with her dress code. My outfit broke a lot of her rules. Bare shoulders. Leggings. Inappropriately tight.

Distracting. I zip up Colby's sweatshirt again. I hate that Matt did this to me, but I can't undo it. My body feels dangerous.

Not so long ago, Vivi, Knox, and I wandered all over town on our own. It's weird to think I'm less safe now than I was when I was little.

I pull out the loose black linen pants Mom bought when she visited somewhere hot and a long black T-shirt I got for a Halloween costume. I won't look like me, but maybe that's just as well.

Then I brush my teeth and wash my face and climb into bed with my clothes still on and read my book under my sheet.

An hour later, my phone buzzes. It's Vivi, saying she's coming up. On my way to the door, I turn off the lights I put on all over the house, so she doesn't think I've lost it.

"What are you doing here?" I ask, wondering if Colby said something—more than that I was sick.

"I felt bad because your mom's not here. And your dad freaks out when you get sick. Is that why you're staying up here?"

I'm embarrassed to tell her what happened, but I'm so grateful she's here. I throw my arms around her.

She rubs my back and says, "Let's get you into bed." She sounds exactly like her own mom.

When I lie back down, she says, "Aren't you hot? You don't want to take that sweatshirt off?"

I shake my head. "I can't get warm."

Vivi strokes my hair, and my whole body relaxes. Adrenaline crash, probably. "It looks like one Colby has," Vivi says.

"Mmmm," I agree, almost asleep now. "He gave it to me."

"Oh. That was nice."

"Yeah." I nestle into the pillow and let Vivi's hand comfort me into sleep.

✳

In the morning, my sadness is gone, but dread fills the space left behind. I can't believe I have to go to this camp and see Matt. I hate the idea of being around anyone who saw the completely helpless way I reacted, much less the actual person who caused it.

Vivi's still asleep on the daybed, so I creep out to get in the shower. I feel disgusting, like I really was sick. After I put on my baggy black clothes and braid my hair, I go back to the bedroom to see if Vivi wants breakfast. Dad will cook for us if we go downstairs. And if Vivi's there, we can pretend last night never happened.

She's sitting up, my museum binder in her lap. "When were you going to tell me?"

"What?" I say, thinking idiotically that she read about the whistling.

"That you got the science camp. You let me think you were doing art."

Right. I completely forgot that part. "Prisha got the art camp," I say, somehow thinking she'll take it better if she thinks someone got something I wanted.

"Prisha. It must be so fun for you. All your friends."

"Vivi?" My voice breaks a little. She has never, ever talked to me like this.

"You need to decide if we're friends. Best friends. Because if we are, I shouldn't have to act like an investigative reporter to figure out what's going on in your life. Lying to your parents is sad, but I get it. But I don't want to be one more person you're afraid of getting in trouble with. I already have a little sister."

I draw in a shuddery breath, trying not to cry. Vivi winces and then steels herself. She's not giving in.

"I didn't tell you about the camp because I didn't want to hurt your feelings," I say.

"It's not just that. You weren't sick last night. You were heartbroken. And now you're dressed like some kind of sad poet, and I have no idea what's going on. If this is one of those growing-apart things, because you want new friends or to go to ordinary high school or to hang out with Prisha instead of me, just say so."

"We're not growing apart," I say. That's the one thing I'm sure of. Although I guess there is kind of a lot I haven't told her.

"Yes, we are. But I can't make you talk. No matter what wish I make."

She looks at me, waiting, but I don't know where to begin. Her shoulders slump, and she grabs her bag. "I'll see you around, I guess."

"Vivi, this isn't fair."

"Tell me about it."

CHAPTER 19

Not a Big Deal

Dad gives me sideways looks on our walk to the museum, clearly wondering what the heck is going on but afraid to ask. I'm happy for the silence.

"Your mother will be home this afternoon."

"What was she doing anyway?"

"I'll let her tell you."

"Right."

"I do know this is hard for you."

"I'm okay," I say.

Disappointed as I am with him, I take Dad's hand when we get to the entrance. Knox and a couple of other kids are up ahead, but I feel like I need a parent. Dad gives me a surprised look.

"Will you walk me in today?"

His eyes widen. "Lilla. What's going on? Did Knox say something to you last night? Or this Colby?"

"No, Dad. Stop calling him 'this Colby.' Forget whatever Vivi's mom said. Colby's great." I hate hearing that suspicion in his voice after everything Colby did yesterday. "There's just a lot of high-school kids and college students…"

"You're almost a high-school student yourself."

"I know. But not yet."

"I guess I should be glad for every minute you're willing to be my little girl. Come on."

We get through the hallway without running into Matt. I say goodbye to Dad and go into the science museum on my own.

"Hey, Lilla," Aman says when I walk into the lab tucked in back. Aman's a high-school senior and one of the head science counselors. From what I saw yesterday, he seems okay.

Excitement about being here starts to dampen some of my worry. I've made slime and terrariums and volcanoes in this room for camps and birthday parties, and now I get to be in charge.

"We're setting up for electricity experiments today," Aman says. "We were thinking you and Drew could work on the circuit puzzles."

"Sound good," I say, moving over to the jumble of wires, batteries, and circuit boards on the table.

"You test the batteries and sort through this stuff," Drew

says to me. "I'll design the puzzles."

I look at him but don't move.

"New plan," Aman says into the silence. "Lilla and I will do the puzzles. Drew, go help Caden."

Drew shrugs. "Whatever."

Together, Aman and I sort through the box, reorganizing and testing. After working in silence for about thirty minutes, he says, "I don't know if it makes you feel any better, but he's like that with everyone. Yesterday, he explained binary to me and Caden."

It does make me feel better. Aman won some kind of coding competition last year. Our computer science teacher had his picture on the wall.

"So it's not a specific form of jerkwaddery. There's something for everyone."

Aman laughs. "Exactly. Although I won't sit here and tell you being a girl has nothing to do with it."

"Thanks," I say. Because I don't like to think I'm imagining it.

After we get everything organized, we work on setting up light-bulb puzzles. We're arguing about how to arrange them from easiest to hardest when Matt comes into the room.

I keep my eyes on the circuit in front of me, making a bigger show of connecting the wires than I need to.

"Can I talk to you a minute, Lilla?" he calls.

Without looking up, I say, "We're a little busy here."

"It'll only take a second."

The light bulb I'm using to test the connections slips out of my hands.

"I need her to finish this up," Aman answers for me. "We'll see you at lunch."

The door closes, but I keep my eyes on the table in front me, brushing the broken glass into a pile.

"What happened?" Aman asks, his voice flat.

"What do you mean?"

"I have some experience getting the crap beat out of me, so I know what afraid looks like."

"It's stupid," I say. It's hard to imagine anyone understanding how I felt yesterday. If you say it out loud, it seems like nothing. And I barely know Aman. And he's a guy.

He pushes back from the table. "Do you want me to get Kate?"

"No!"

His eyes get bigger. Drew and Caden show up at the door. "Ready for lunch?" Caden says.

"In a minute," Aman answers, not taking his eyes off me. "You go ahead."

They leave.

"I'm sorry. But it's not just about you. He works at a camp for kids. You need to tell me what happened. Or I can get Molly or Kate, but we need to know what we're dealing with here."

Aman's thinking this is worse than it is. And he's sweet to

offer to get Molly or Kate, but I'd rather tell him. I like how comfortable he is with silence and that he stood up for me with Drew and that he won't let this go. Before I bring in an adult, I'd like to run it by someone closer to my age.

I tell him the story.

Disgust crosses Aman's face. "You're a kid."

I shrug, thinking about what I was wearing and feeling guilty. "I don't think he knew that. At first."

Aman looks at the empty doorway. "My guess is he wants to apologize. You want to let him?"

"I don't know. I don't want to be alone with him."

"If you want to hear what he has to say, I can be there."

"Thank you," I say. I'd rather deal with Matt with company than have him seek me out when I'm alone. I'm not afraid exactly. But definitely uncomfortable.

Aman and I walk down to the windowless basement cafeteria with its row of ancient vending machines. A long time ago, someone painted polka dots on the walls to try to cheer the place up. They did not succeed.

Knox, Colby, and Prisha are all sitting at a round table. Matt's not in the room.

"Saved you a spot!" Prisha says, smiling. She seems to have gotten over me not going home with her yesterday.

"Feeling better, Lilla?" Knox asks. He tilts his head. "On second thought, you don't look that great."

Prisha shoves his shoulder. "Be nice."

"Was that not nice?" he asks, looking confused. "Because she's not normally so pale and vampire-like."

"I'm okay." I put my lunch on the table.

"Lilla and I have to go see Matt," Aman says. "Be right back."

It's just as well. There's no way I can eat right now. I barely ate breakfast, and I had trouble keeping that down. I can't imagine the evolutionary reason for this. How is throwing up a useful response to stress?

Matt and Molly are in the classroom where I interviewed. He jumps up when he sees us, and my whole body freezes. Just like on the street yesterday. I can't stop seeing his face when I turned around. I've read the word *leer* a couple of times, but I didn't know what it looked like until yesterday.

"I need to check in with these two about something. You want to go down for lunch?" Matt says to Molly as he opens the door for her. He looks at Aman. "Can you give us a minute? I need to talk with Lilla."

Worried, I turn to Aman, but he doesn't move. "Lilla wants me to stay."

I nod.

"It's a glassed-in room. He'll be able to see everything from the hall," Matt says, still holding the door.

I find my voice. "No."

Matt runs his hand through his hair and steps away from the door. "You told him?"

I nod again.

"God. You look terrified. I'm so sorry. I never would have done that if I had known."

"Known what?" I ask.

"That you were so young."

How old would have made it okay? Fourteen? Sixteen? I don't say this out loud. Because, as nice as Aman's been, that's what he said too. That it wasn't okay because I was a kid. But is that really the only reason it was wrong?

"From the back, you didn't look thirteen."

"Twelve," I say.

His face turns pale. But then he says, "In some ways, it's a compliment. Lots of girls would feel flattered."

I glance at Aman, wanting—I'm not sure what—to have someone else disagree, I guess.

Aman gives Matt a tight smile. "I don't think she was flattered."

I was not. And I am not now, even though I'm safe. The fear of what might have happened is still much too fresh. My head tells me I should yell at Matt right now. I can even think of things to say. *There were two of you. I didn't know what might happen next. I will always be afraid now.* But I don't know how to be that person.

"It would be best if you stayed away from Lilla," Aman says, breaking the silence. "There's no reason for you to be involved with the science camp. Molly's in engineering. She should supervise us anyway."

Matt gets all offended. "I don't know what she told you, but it wasn't a big deal. I'm not a predator."

"Dude. You're in college and you're whistling at middle-school girls. You don't like the label, you might want to reconsider the behavior."

They glare at each other. Then Matt throws up his hands. "Fine. I'm done here."

After Matt leaves, Aman asks, "You okay?"

"Yes. Thank you," I say. I am so grateful. Knowing I won't have to deal with Matt while I'm here is a huge relief.

But I'm uneasy too. Because this was my second chance to tell Matt what I thought of him. To take control. And I didn't do any better.

I'm not sure what's wrong with me.

CHAPTER 20

Troubled

After lunch, Aman puts me in charge of setting up static-electricity experiments. It's quiet and uncomplicated work.

Unfortunately.

Because now I have to think.

About Vivi and how she is sad and angry because I kept secrets from her.

About Matt and how I didn't stand up to him. Twice.

About Mom and Dad, who are keeping secrets from me and who will be so Disappointed in Me if I don't become a magnet school kid.

And also about Knox, who, all of a sudden, I'm afraid to talk to and I can't bring myself to tell him why because it might hurt his feelings if I say I don't like him, or worse, if I say I do like him but don't want to do anything about it because I'm afraid now. What if he thinks I'm afraid of him?

But then, maybe he likes Vivi and not me.

In that case, I guess it wouldn't bother him at all if I didn't like him. And even though I don't want to do anything about it now, thinking he likes her instead of me still makes me sad, which I know doesn't make any sense, but there it is.

I'd like to blame all this on Matt, but it started long before yesterday.

All my life I have worked to keep everyone happy. Vivi and Knox and my teachers and especially Mom and Dad. I have done all the things they asked me to do, and all the things they barely hinted they wanted. Good grades. Gymnastics. Drawing. Photography. Coding. Accelerated English. Advanced math.

And even when they got divorced and moved me out of the house I grew up in and made me wonder why I wasn't enough to keep together two people who still liked each other enough to sit at a kitchen table and laugh, I didn't complain.

But it wasn't enough. And maybe it's never going to be? No matter how many tests I ace or magnet schools I get into or science fairs I win. Maybe I can never be smart or ambitious or sweet or charming enough to make them happy?

And this thing with Matt. Sure, I don't like that guys are

out there waiting to say stuff about my body. But more, I hate that I was so afraid of upsetting Matt—of not being *nice*—that I didn't talk back.

But I don't know how to be different.

Only then I remember that yes, yes I do.

I told Mrs. Wilder I didn't want to talk about what I was reading even though I knew she might not be happy.

Why?

Maybe because I didn't have to yell, but mostly because of Vivi. I cared more about what Vivi thought than about what Mrs. Wilder thought. Maybe in some anti-peer-pressure-school-assembly kind of way, I shouldn't care what anyone thinks, but I don't see that happening. And what I know for sure is that caring what Vivi thinks of me makes me stronger and braver.

I need to say sorry for not telling her I got the science museum. And I need to tell her what happened with Matt. And when I do, I want to be able to say I talked to Kate. Because that's what Vivi will expect. And because it's right.

When I let Aman know I'm going to talk to Kate, he says, "Thank Joss Whedon and all the Agents of S.H.I.E.L.D. There was no way I could let you leave without doing that, but I'm glad I don't have to march you down there."

When Kate sees me at her door, she waves me in. Feeling almost as dizzy as I did last night, I sort of fall into the seat across from her.

"Do you not feel well?" she asks. "Should we get your dad?"

I shake my head. "I need to tell you something."

When she settles back, I tell her the story, leaving out my "'Kay?" and the dash across the street.

Kate pulls a tissue out of a box on her desk and hands it to me, but I'm not crying.

"Are you sure it was Matt?"

"Yes. He apologized today."

"Oh! Well, good." She's a lot less upset than Aman.

"Good?" I ask, trying to sort through my feelings. I expected more outrage. If anything, I thought I'd be the one telling her not to overreact.

"It sounds like a misunderstanding. You were dressed for a party?"

"Not a party," I say, but I hear the doubt in my voice, and so does she.

"Remember, we talked about this?"

The dress-code stuff, she means.

"What did your parents say?" she asks.

"Oh, I haven't told them yet. My mom's out of town, and my dad..." My voice trails off.

"I understand," Kate says. "It's hard to talk to fathers about this sort of thing. And you've told me. No need to make a big production out of it."

"I guess," I say, surprised. Most adults—even near-adults like Aman and spirit-adults like Vivi—seem to push for telling the whole story. It's weird to have a legit grown-up tell me it's okay to keep quiet. "I suppose this sort of thing happens all the time?"

Kate smiles. "I'm afraid it does. He shouldn't have whistled at you, but boys…"

She gives me a what-can-you-do shrug.

So I guess that's that.

CHAPTER 21

Totally Normal

At the end of the day, Knox runs into the science museum. "Lilla, come see!"

Despite everything, I smile. He is lit up.

Aman sends me off with a promise that it will be okay. Knox gives me a curious look, but I ignore it. Knox still thinks Matt is a Cool Guy, and I don't want to get into it.

In the main hall of the children's museum, blue and yellow foam blocks are stacked to make a giant Jenga game that towers way over my head. The only way to reach the top is to climb the tree house or the pirate ship on either side.

"Want to play?" Knox says, bouncing on his toes.

Joy washes over me. "Yes! Did you and Colby build this?"

Knox nods. "But he had to go. Min and Garrett have to finish some paperwork, and they said we could try it out while they were working. This is going to be the first thing we do with the kids."

I'm jealous. Our first activity is picking up puffballs with static electricity.

I scramble up the netting of the pirate ship, sliding one hand through the holes to anchor myself before I lean way over to slide out one of the blocks in the middle.

"Careful," Knox says below me, looking nervous.

"You're planning to do this with little children," I remind him.

"Maybe we need to scale back?"

"Come on! Get up here!" I answer. I used to climb ropes to the gym ceiling. I'm not worried.

Knox climbs the ladder to the tree house, leans out the window, and nudges out a block from the other side. The tower holds.

I crawl out onto the top of the monkey bars that connect the ship to the tree house. Then I push out another block with my foot. Everything wobbles.

Knox joins me, but instead of reaching for the safest bet, he kicks at one of the corner blocks.

"Knox!" I say as everything tumbles down. The blocks collapse into a giant mountain below us. I'm tempted to jump into them, but one time I did that with snow, and it turned out to be a lot harder than I expected. I glare at Knox. "You did that on purpose."

"I wanted to see what would happen."

We sit in silence on the monkey bars, swinging our feet.

"I'm glad we got to do this together." Knox's voice is quiet but intense. "The camps, I mean. Not the blocks."

"Me too." My eyes are still on the foam mountain below, and I'm too nervous to turn my head. I don't want to see Knox looking at me the way Matt did.

That night by the river, I thought I wanted to find out what it would be like for Knox and me to be more than friends. But after what happened with Matt, I don't anymore. I'm used to Knox seeing me as Lilla. A whole person he can talk to about his parents' divorce and his music and our love of chocolate. I don't want him to look at me like some girl-shaped thing…who he wants to do who knows what with.

Knox's fingers brush against mine, and I yelp, flinging myself off the monkey bars and down into the foam.

Because I'm going to be totally normal around him.

Obviously.

Without speaking, I busy myself restacking blocks. Knox, after getting down the regular way, joins in. I can feel him watching me, but he doesn't speak. I'm not sure how to make this awkwardness between us disappear. And I'm out of places to throw myself.

We rebuild a tower not quite as tall as the old one, and go get Min and Garret to approve.

Once we're out on the front steps, Knox asks if I want to meet Vivi at the bakery before we go home.

"Yes!" This is perfect. My individual awkwardness with each of them will cancel the other out. Like multiplying negative numbers. But I'm not totally sure Vivi will answer me. "Can you text her?"

Knox tilts his head. And the gesture is so familiar, so his, that something in me warms. And that must show in my face because he gives me his sweetest smile.

I look away.

When I turn back, he's focused on his phone. "She wants to know if you're going to be there. You want to tell me what's going on between you two?"

I don't know what to say. Knox, Vivi, and I talk about everything, except each other. This is how we hang onto this three-sided friendship.

"Things have been weird lately. Because of the museum. And school next year. And Prisha. All of a sudden Vivi's all jealous of her."

Knox raises his eyebrows. "Are you sure it's Prisha she's jealous of?"

"What do you mean?"

He stops, but instead of looking at me, he examines his red shoes. "It's okay. Just say it."

Uh-oh. Maybe Knox knows. How I was thinking about him. And he thinks Vivi is jealous of us. This is so, so embarrassing.

Especially since it's all different for me now. I don't want to deal with any of it.

"Lilla?" Knox nudges my shoe with his foot. "However this works out, we'll still be friends."

"What are you talking about?"

Knox raises his head. "Colby?"

Now I'm confused. "Why are we talking about Colby?"

"Because you both like him."

"Who?"

"You and Vivi."

"We do?"

"Don't you?"

I giggle, and a smile creeps onto Knox's face.

"I don't *not* like Colby. But I don't *like* like him." After last night, I'm grateful for Colby, but I can tell that's not what Knox means.

"He wouldn't say what happened with you the other night, even though Vivi kept bugging him. She told me he gave you his sweatshirt and you kept it, and I wasn't trying to eavesdrop, but I thought you said his name with your dad this morning before you came into the museum."

"I kept his sweatshirt because I blew my nose in it," I explain. "I tried to give it back, but he didn't want it. And I don't remember what I said this morning, but it was probably that Colby isn't an ax murderer, and my dad should stop thinking you two are trying to corrupt me and Vivi."

Knox's smile grows huge. "Okay then." He bumps my shoulder with his.

Uh-oh. I might have overcorrected here.

"Why do you think Vivi likes Colby?" I ask.

"Because I have eyes."

"Even if you're right, you have the accuracy of a coin flip." Given how wrong he was about me, he doesn't need to make it seem like he's some kind of crush oracle.

"My judgment might be…clouded when it comes to you."

I don't want to think about his clouded judgment, so I think about Vivi. Maybe Vivi does like Colby and thinks I do, too, and that I've been keeping this from her, along with everything else. That's why she asked if I was telling other lies to her and Knox and why she was so mad this morning after she saw me in his sweatshirt. This part, at least, will be easy to fix.

"Come on," I say and take off toward the bakery, eager to make things right.

"Don't tell her I told you," he says, following me. "She'll murder me."

When we get to Cookie Mistake, Knox jumps in front of me to grab the door, even though I was there first.

I knock his hand off the handle because I am in no mood. "I am completely capable of opening a door."

"Drama queen, much?" he says, not moving out of the way.

My emotions are all over the place. This storm cloud rising

in me isn't about Knox. Not really. But he's the one in front of me, treating me like I'm helpless.

"When you do something for me that I can easily do myself, I feel like you think I can't do anything. Because I'm a girl."

"Me holding the door for you is not me saying that you—or all the girls in the world—can't enter restaurants without my help. You think Vivi would let me walk around if she thought I didn't believe girls could open doors?"

"Vivi!" I say. Because it always comes back to this. *Don't act like a girl* turns into *Don't act like Lilla.* "Just because I like pink and am a little quiet and want to be in color guard instead playing soccer doesn't mean it's okay for you to take over. I am not a Cotton Candy Princess."

He smirks. "You are dressed like you're going to someone's funeral. You couldn't look less like a princess. I was being polite. For a friend."

"Are you telling me you would have jumped in front of Colby to open that door?" I'm not raising my voice, but I want to be right a little more than I usually do. I'm mad, but, weirdly, a little grateful too. Because Knox is the only person I feel safe enough with to fight with like this.

"I. Was. Being. A. Gentleman." Knox is maybe not so much sensing my gratitude.

A woman behind us clears her throat. I turn to her. "Could you please give us a minute?" I say. "I am educating him, and it's important."

"You are blocking the door," she angry whispers.

"Sorry," I say. It's clear she thinks her need for a lopsided baked good is more important than whatever we have going on here. I take an exaggerated step to the side, but when I gesture dramatically toward the door, I smack the stroller she's pushing, which makes the baby under the canopy wail. The woman glares at me, and I leap back. "Sorry. Sorry. I was only trying to make a point. I didn't mean to wake your baby."

With a sarcastic look at me, Knox leaps to open the door for her.

The woman says "Thank you" to him and pushes her stroller inside.

"Well?" Knox says, still holding the door.

His hidden smile makes my own want to break out, but I won't let it. "I can't go in there now!"

He lets the door close. "You're right. The crying baby is sort of a downside." He's trying very hard not to laugh. "I'll tell Vivi to meet us at With a Twist instead."

CHAPTER 22

Best Friends

When we get to the frozen yogurt store, Knox puts his hands behind his back. "Go in however you think is best."

I pull the door open. "After you."

He goes inside but can't leave it alone. "Thank you. Somehow that didn't make me feel like you didn't think I could get in on my own."

I scowl. "It's not the same."

"Why not?"

I haven't thought this through, so I'm not sure, but it definitely has to do with knowing Knox is never going to get whistled at while walking down the street.

"Look, I get you were trying to be nice, but when you jump in front of me to grab a door, you make me feel like a girl first and Lilla second."

"I can think of you as both Lilla and a girl. I do it all the time. And besides, you holding the door for me didn't make me feel like you thought of me as just some guy."

I take a deep breath, trying to find words that will make sense to him. "It's different. You holding the door for me is part of a whole thing. Hundreds of years of history that say that I can't do basic things. Because I'm a girl."

"So I should never hold a door for you?"

"No. If you get there first, you can hold the door, but if I'm already there, don't push me out of the way to show how polite you are."

"Actually, when you say it like that, it sounds pretty reasonable."

Vivi comes through the door. "Why aren't we at the bakery?"

"Lilla got mad at me and caused a ruckus," Knox says. "We had to leave."

"What did you do?" She doesn't look at me. We are not okay yet.

"I held the door for her."

"You monster," she says and goes to get her yogurt.

"Should I leave?" Knox says as we follow. "Seems like you two have some stuff to work out."

"I won't send you away without food," I say. "But maybe leave early? We had a fight this morning. We need to talk."

"You had a fight with Vivi too?" He whistles. "Lilla on the rampage."

I smile, but it's half-hearted. When I have a hard time falling asleep, I remind myself of everything that works in my life. There's one thing always on this list: Vivi and Knox are my best friends. I need to fix this.

At the table, Knox plows through his frozen yogurt at a speed that's surprising even for him, and claims he has to go.

Vivi jumps up, holding her cup. "Me too! I'll walk you out."

"Vivi," I say. "Please. Stay." I fight to keep my voice even. I don't want her to do it because she feels guilty.

Knox puts his hands on Vivi's shoulders. "Sit down, Viv. Whatever happened, you need to work this out. My life doesn't make sense when you two are fighting."

Vivi sits back down and stirs her yogurt. She likes it half-melted. "Well?"

"I need to tell you something."

She raises her eyebrows again.

"Fine," I say. "I need to tell you some *things*. You might not like them."

She doesn't tell me it will be okay, but I plunge in anyway. I have to trust her, or what's the point?

"You will always be my best friend. I hope. But I want to be friends with Prisha too. I've been telling her I don't want to hang out. Because of you. But I want to do things with her sometimes. It doesn't mean I'm trying to replace you. I couldn't."

Vivi's quiet, but I can tell it's thinking quiet, not angry quiet.

"I'm worried about high school," she says. "If you don't come, everything's going to change. What if that's the end of us?"

"I don't think it will be. You hang out with your soccer friends, and I used to spend all that time with gymnastics girls, and we were still best friends." In my head though, I'm less sure. My parents thought they would be together forever. Until they didn't. I don't know what this means for me and Vivi, except that my life needs to be a little bigger than her and Knox. Just in case.

"I don't want to be one of those girls who says you can only have one friend. But I don't like it when you shut me out."

"We don't have to do everything together to stay friends, even best friends," I say.

"I know. But you have to talk to me."

"I will. This Summer Wish…it's good. You were right. I need to not be so afraid to talk to people. Especially you."

She squeezes my hand. "You know I love you."

"I love you too, Vivi."

She comes across the table to hug me. We stay like that a long time, and when we break apart, I'm a little embarrassed. We're usually not so over-the-top with our feelings.

"So," she says with a little laugh. "What's next on your list of things to tell me?"

"Colby?"

"Okay." She grips the bottom of her chair. Like she's bracing for impact.

"I don't like Colby," I say.

"How can you not like Colby?" she asks, all offended. Knox was so right.

"I mean, he's great," I say with a grin.

Vivi narrows her eyes.

"For you."

"How did you figure it out?" Her mouth drops open. "Is it obvious? Do you think he knows?"

Given that Knox is the one who told me, that's a big yes, but I don't want to embarrass her. "What are you going to do?"

"I'm not doing anything else. He needs to do something. Why won't he? I'm adorable."

"So adorable," I agree. Waiting for him doesn't seem like the Vivi way. "What about telling the truth? Being brave?"

"I was already brave. It's his turn," she says stubbornly. "I've been flirting and flirting with him and I can't tell if he likes me at all. Plus, he's giving other girls his sweatshirt."

"Sorry about that," I say. "But I want you to know that even if I did like Colby, I never could have liked him enough to let him come between us. He's just a boy."

"A cute boy."

"Even so."

"I wouldn't let him come between us either," says Vivi. "I was going to let you have him."

"That's sweet, but I don't want him. And Colby might want to, you know, express an opinion?"

"No hope of that," Vivi says. "Sorry, I flipped out about his sweatshirt."

I shake my head. "I didn't even realize what that was about until…" I stop. I don't want to throw Knox under the bus. "I thought you were mad about the science museum."

"Well, I was. It was weird you didn't tell me. I felt like you didn't trust me or you didn't need me—because now you were going to be friends with Prisha instead."

"It's not instead. I will always need you."

"Good."

"And I have to tell you one more thing."

"More?" she asks.

"Unfortunately."

CHAPTER 23

Boys Being Boys

Vivi and I sit on a bench across the street from Matt's fraternity house. A bunch of guys throw a football around in the front yard. My whole body feels the way it used to before a big meet—palms sweaty, skin electric, heart pounding. I force myself to take the deep breaths my coach taught us to do to calm down.

Even with the street and the trees around us, I'm a little afraid Matt will recognize me, but I want Vivi to see.

She gives me more time than I expect before pushing me. "Why are we here?"

"One of the assistant directors for the museum camps lives over there."

Vivi looks at me carefully. I go back to watching across the street. A group of college girls go by, and one of the guys yells something. One of the girls yells something back. Not bothered. But half a block away, a girl alone crosses to the other side of the street so she doesn't have to walk in front of the house. Which I will do. Every time I come this way. For the rest of my life.

"When I was on my way over to see you all the other night, he whistled at me."

Vivi turns toward me, and I shift so we're sitting cross-legged, knees touching, heads close together. It makes it easy to talk quietly.

"He didn't know who I was," I go on. "He said to come back in a few years."

"What did you do?"

"Nothing." I give a sad laugh. "I ran away. I cried. Colby found me and gave me his sweatshirt."

"Oh, that's why…" Vivi says.

I nod. "And today, when I let him apologize—Matt, not Colby—he said I should think of it like a compliment."

"Not a great time for me to start a fight, huh?"

"You couldn't have known."

"Yeah. That's kind of been my point. Why didn't you tell me?"

I lift a shoulder. "Too embarrassed. Because it happened. And because of the way I reacted."

"You're not the one who should be embarrassed."

"When he told me to come back, I laughed, Vivi. You would have punched him in the face. That's why I couldn't tell you. I'm bad at being brave."

Vivi does a sad smile. "I wouldn't have hit him. The first time it happened to me, I cried too."

"The first time?" What on earth? Not only did she not tell me, but there's been more than one time?

"I was with my mom," Vivi continues. "Some guy yelled something awful out a car window at both of us."

"How many times has it happened?"

"Three." She taps my leg. "I know you may not get this, but all this stuff is worse when you're not white. How often it happens and what they say."

"Why didn't you tell me?"

She shrugs. "I didn't want to worry you. You don't like talking about anything like this."

She's right. I'm sure that's part of the reason she didn't want to tell me about Colby. I'm pretty private. Even with Vivi.

"What are you doing here?" I jump at the voice next to us, and my head smacks Vivi's.

It's Matt. I can't believe I let him get so close without noticing.

I scramble to my feet. Vivi follows. Even so, we're looking up at him. I take a step back.

"When I apologized today, I meant it," he says. "But I am not going to let you destroy my summer. You need to get over it. Aman's treating me like a criminal, and I'm supposed to be in charge."

Boo-hoo, I think, but do not say. To my credit, I also don't tell him that it's okay. Part of me wants to though. Say the right words and make everything go back the way it was. Vivi doesn't speak, but she edges closer to me so our shoulders touch.

"This wasn't a big deal. I get you're young. But it's not like guys don't do this all the time. Grow up and move on."

He goes back across the street.

"You need to tell Kate," Vivi says when he's gone. "He can't get away with this."

"Come on," I say, pulling her hand. I want to get away from here. Once we're headed back toward my house, I say, "I did tell Kate."

"What did she say?"

"That she would talk to him. And it was just boys being boys."

We walk in silence for a while.

"Do you think that could be true? That it is just boys being boys, I mean?" Vivi asks.

"I don't know. I can't imagine Knox or Colby doing it. But maybe they're different when they're not with us?"

Vivi's silent for a while. Finally, she says, "No. I won't believe that. And I think guys like Matt know it's a big deal. They pretend it's a compliment about how you look, but really, they like that girls are scared."

"I wish I wasn't," I say.

Vivi takes my hand. "I know. Me too."

CHAPTER 24

Best for Me

That night Vivi sends me a link to a website about street harassment. I like the words—*street harassment*. I mean, I don't enjoy them, but they feel more like what happened to me than *catcalling*. That sounds a little silly.

And all the numbers. I'm amazed. By seventeen, it happens to almost all of us. So many girls say the first time was when they were eleven. Or even younger. *What is wrong with people?* One in four girls have been touched while they're out in public. The stories make me glad I live in small town without any public buses or subways. They seem awful.

I read story after story. They feel so familiar. The shock and embarrassment. The wanting to escape. I read that girls who blame themselves or who respond passively—like me— feel worse afterward. We are more afraid and more likely to worry about where we can walk and what we can wear.

Mom knocks on my bedroom door.

I flip my laptop shut. "Come in."

She spent dinner not talking and scrolling through her phone. That suited me fine. I'm still angry with Dad, but I'm not feeling all that cozy with her either. I need to make nice though because I want to sleep up here.

It's one thing for Dad to start dating. I don't love the idea, but I get that it was going to happen. But it's something else for him to flat-out lie to me about it when I was standing right there. I don't want to feel uncertain all the time.

But I'm not starting this talk. That's his job. So if he thinks I want more nights up here because I need time with Mom, I'm good with that. As long as I get my way.

Mom sits on my bed. "Can I talk to you about something?"

Uh-oh.

Something is never ice cream or bookstores or Disney World. It's always your math test or the divorce or the dozen toads discovered in the washing machine because you and your two best friends thought they needed a damp environment. You know, hypothetically.

"Sure?"

"That trip I took. To Northwestern? It went really well."

"Congratulations?" I'm not sure what she's getting at here. Mom doesn't usually need me to tell her she did a good job at work.

"They offered me a job. It's a yearlong visiting position right now, but it could turn into more."

It's almost eighty degrees outside, and my window's open, but all at once I'm ice cold. My mind races. How far is Northwestern? Four hours? And a whole other state? No. It's not fair to ask this. Not right before eighth grade.

"I can't move to Chicago." I don't say this as a question. I'm that sure.

She shakes her head. "No, no. I wouldn't ask that of you. I can go down Sunday nights. Come back Fridays. You'd stay with your dad. And during breaks, you can live upstairs full time, so we can catch up."

My dad. The one with the secret girlfriend.

"Why?" I whisper. How does this make sense? Is it to get away from him? Couldn't we just move to the other side of town like Knox's dad? I'd be all for that. Unless it's to get away from me. I know I haven't been so easy to be around these last few weeks. Am I too much for her now?

"It's a much, much better school. More support for research, better labs, colleagues who push my thinking. It could be game-changing for my career. Even if it's short term."

"But what about me?" My voice sounds small. It's one thing to think that maybe I'm not the center of my parents' lives, but it's something else for her to thrust the evidence in front of me like this.

"In another five years, you'll be off to college. I wish I

could wait, but I can't pass up an opportunity this good and this close."

Mom has never been completely happy here. I know that. But I thought it was mostly because she wanted to spend more time traveling the world looking for bugs, not that she wanted to work somewhere else. Live somewhere else. She's made noises about moving before, but Dad always ended all that by talking about what was Best for Me. Then I get it. All at once.

"This is why you got divorced."

After a few seconds of silence, she says, "A divorce never has one reason." But I'm right. Dad will never leave his museum or his garden or his familiar life. And she wanted to move away as soon as I finished high school. Only now she doesn't have to wait. Because she can leave me here with him. And he can find someone who's happy to stay.

Good for them, I guess.

The back door of Mom's place opens, and Mom and I look at each other, united in a sharp flash of fear. Only it must be Dad. To make it easier for me to go back and forth, we leave our back doors open. Just the one to the outside at the bottom of the stairs stays locked all the time. Still, Dad's never walked into Mom's house without knocking.

Dad comes into my room and looks between us.

"You told her," he says. When Mom nods, he adds, "What do you say, kiddo? Can you survive weekdays with me?"

His hands are in his pockets, and he looks more relaxed than either Mom or me. Sure of my answer. Enjoying his chance to be the good parent.

I remember Knox snarling at his father when they came into the auditorium, and I wish I could do that. I want to hurt them both. Tell Mom it's not fair to leave me when the whole world is getting so scary and confusing. Tell Dad not to smile at me like we are so, so close. But I can't bring myself to do it.

Instead I say, "What does your girlfriend think about you being a full-time parent?"

Dad looks at Mom. "You told her? Why?"

"It wasn't Mom." He puts his eyes back on me. "I heard you on the phone. The other night."

His face changes. Remembering. Deciding all my upset was because of him. Good. Let him think that.

"I told you that you shouldn't have hid this from her," Mom says. "That she needs to know what's going on. This move is going to be hard enough without her having to worry that you're sneaking around."

Her anger warms me a little, but I can't help but notice she made this about her awfully fast. And she doesn't seem to remember that she hid something from me too.

"Can you leave? Both of you."

"I'm sorry, Lilla. I thought it was for the best," Dad says. "There was no reason for you to know about..." He stops.

"Say it," I say. "Her name."

"Dana."

"Dana?" Mom says. "I thought her name was Julie."

He looks up into the corner of the room. "Lilla heard me on the phone with Dana. But it's not serious, so…"

"So?" I say, not sure how I'm supposed to fill in that blank.

"So, I'm seeing a couple of people."

"Gross." I know I can't expect my parents to be alone for the rest of their lives, but I definitely didn't expect this. Dad is old. One person should be plenty.

"This is a lot to take in," Mom says to me. Her voice is short. She's angry with Dad but trying not to take it out on me. "But you'll get through this. Next year you'll still be in middle school. It'll be fine. And if you need me back for high school to help you through the science track, I'll do it. No questions asked."

Before I can figure out how to answer—because hard classes aren't what I'm worried about—Dad says, "The science track? I thought the arts program was your first choice. I may not be good for much, but I can help with that."

"What are you talking about?" Mom looks at me. I open my mouth but can't think what to say. Mom reads my face. "Oh, Lilla. Please tell me this isn't about Knox. That you're not going to decide what to do with the rest of your life because you want a boyfriend."

I shake my head, unable to believe how off track she is.

She dismissed me and what I want so quickly. Not even giving me a chance to say I want to go to a school without Knox or Vivi. Because it's best for me.

"You're twelve. You can't have a boyfriend," Dad says. "And why did you say Knox? What about this Colby?"

"Dad," I say. "Please stop calling him 'this Colby.'"

"See," Dad says to Mom.

"Way to focus on what's important, Will," Mom says.

He glares at her.

I need my life to stop for a minute. This is. All. Too. Much. I close my eyes and put my hands over my ears until they're quiet.

When I open my eyes, I say, "Can you not? Tonight? Can you give me one night when I don't have to worry about what you want or how to make you happy?" My throat's closing because I'm holding back tears, but I manage to get out the words.

"Lilla," Mom says. She's hurt. But I'm out. I have nothing left to comfort her with.

"That's not fair," Dad says. "We've organized our whole lives around you."

"No. You organized your lives so you can do what you want without feeling bad about it. And I do coding and art and tutoring and gifted classes because you think I should." I wish my voice could be louder and stronger, but I'm too close to falling apart to manage anything above a whisper. "I am applying to the magnet school. And I sleep where you tell me, and I don't have a single space anywhere in the whole world that feels like mine. And I will be doing this for the rest of my life because Christmas and Thanksgiving and my birthday will always be organized around the two of you and where you are and what you want. And tomorrow, I will be ready to pretend that it's fine again. That it's no big deal that Mom wants to live away from me five days a week and that Dad is…doing whatever he's doing. But right now, I need you to leave the room I am sleeping in tonight."

Mom and Dad say nothing. They look stunned. I can see Dad thinking about whether to tell me to go downstairs, but he doesn't. After they leave, I shut the door behind them and lean against it until the waves of anxiety settle a little.

Then a nervous laugh escapes. I need to text Vivi. I am for sure getting some Summer Wish points for this, even if she didn't make it a challenge.

CHAPTER 25

Do Science, Draw Pictures, Smile Sweetly

That night I barely sleep. I'm obsessed with the new feeling curling inside me. I told my parents how I felt, and it was scary, but the world didn't end. It's like after the library with Mrs. Wilder, but times ten.

Mom and Dad whisper-argued in the kitchen for a while. And then they went to bed. They're still my parents. Mom will go to Chicago or she won't. Dad will talk to me about who he's dating or he won't. I'll go to the magnet school or I won't. We'll find a way through this. But for the first time in a year, I'm not alone with my problems.

And I didn't yell or scream or slam doors or do any

of the things I always thought being angry meant. I said how I felt. Quietly. Honestly. Lilla-like.

At breakfast, Mom and I eat our bagels in silence while she watches me carefully. "Do you want to talk about anything?"

"Not yet," I say, but I'm not hiding. I'm thinking. "Vivi invited me to sleep over tonight. Can I go?"

She wants to say no but doesn't feel up to it. Before, I would have seen she didn't like the idea and said never mind, but today I keep my mouth shut until she says, "Sure. But tomorrow, we need to talk. All of us."

"Okay." I know they can't ignore all the things I said last night, and I don't really want them to. But I'm in no hurry to keep talking about them.

When I show up at Vivi's after lunch, I find her and Prisha on the porch playing with Gabi. I sit down by them cautiously.

"What's going on?" I don't know if I should be happy or afraid.

Vivi gives me a hopeful smile. "I asked Prisha to stay over too. Is that okay?"

A grin pushes my cheeks way up. "That's awesome!"

Vivi scoops up Gabi. "I think I've fulfilled my duties as a sister today. I'm going to take her in. Be right back."

"Surprised?" Prisha says when Vivi goes.

"No," I lie. "Vivi thinks you're great."

She snorts, a sound I didn't know she could make. "We

decided that since you like us both, we must be worth the effort."

"Maybe I have terrible taste in friends?"

"Except Knox is such a cinnamon roll."

"Oooo. Are you getting Lilla to talk about Knox?" Vivi hands each of us a lime popsicle and sits down on the steps below us.

"What do you mean?" I ask.

"I figured it out—why you don't like Colby," Vivi says. "It's because you have a crush on Knox."

I hide behind sarcasm. "Because that's the only reason I could not like Colby."

"Why are you so weird about this? He likes you, and not the way he likes me. That doesn't mean you have to like him back, but I think you do?"

Prisha nods with big exaggerated movements.

A little flicker of warmth glows inside me, but I stomp it down. "I don't want it to be like that with Knox. I don't want him to look at me like…"

My voice trails off. Prisha looks confused, but Vivi gets it.

"You can't let that take away something good. It doesn't have to be like that with boys. Knox thinks of you like a person, not a thing."

"He does now," I say. But it's hard for me to believe that will stay the same if he starts thinking about me as a girl-friend. He's already all excited to open doors in a completely unnecessary way.

"What happened?" Prisha asks.

"It wasn't a big thing."

"Don't do that," Vivi says. "It was a big deal. Is a big deal. You work with this person. And so does she. And he's terrible."

I tell Prisha about the catcalling, and she's not surprised. "I stopped walking by the fraternities a long time ago. What did Kate say?" It doesn't even occur to Prisha that I wouldn't have told Kate. Is this how everyone else goes about their lives? Not worrying whether they'll upset other people with their words? Just…saying things?

"She said she'd talk to him," I say. "But…"

"You can't keep working with him. Do you want to quit?"

"No," Vivi says before I can answer. "You haven't even gotten to work with the kids yet. Think of something else."

But I don't see how I can go into the museum every day and see Matt.

"Knox nailed it at the music store this morning. It was sort of sweet, actually," Vivi says, making me wish I could have seen it. "I need to set a new challenge. Maybe you should lead a protest."

For a moment, I imagine leading people up and down the street carrying a sign and chanting. I shake my head. "Not my thing."

"You could tell Matt what you think of him and let him know he'd better stay away from you or else," Prisha says.

"That'd work too," Vivi says.

Telling off Matt feels good in my imagination, but in real life I'd fall apart and feel worse.

"I need a way to be brave that feels like me."

Vivi says, "So, you want to draw pictures, do science, and smile sweetly about street harassment?"

I snap my head toward her.

"What?" she says.

"Yes," I say. "That's what I'm going to do."

CHAPTER 26

Totally Clear

I am the daughter of two PhDs. I may be quiet and not very ambitious, but I can do a research project. Using Vivi's computer, we blow up a map of the blocks around campus.

"We can print this at the university library," I say. "They have one of those giant printers."

"Isn't that expensive?" Vivi asks.

"We can do it in black and white. And it's worth it." When I got the job at the museum camp, Mom and Dad put a hundred dollars in my bank account. They said it was less than they would have spent on the coding camp I was going to do with Vivi if I didn't get picked, and I should get paid for my work. I'm happy to spend some of it on this.

Later we set up in front of the college library, laying our giant map flat on the ground. I have a box of colored sticky dots in my hand.

Summer session's started, and while the campus isn't as crowded as during the school year, it's awake. We're a little giggly at first, but the college girls we talk to are sweet, and pretty soon we have a routine. Prisha goes first, asking students and professors and tourists about the first time they were catcalled. Next, she sends them to me at the map. I explain our color coding—blue for wherever you heard someone say something to you, yellow for anyplace you've been followed, and red for anywhere a stranger's put his hands on you in public. I give out more red dots than I expect. Vivi has them sign a petition to end street harassment around campus.

Clouds of color bloom around the fraternities—not just Matt's—and around a bar downtown and, strangely, in front of a car wash. Almost no one takes only one dot to put on the map. And no one says they can't remember where it happened.

When a woman who's at least Mom's age takes a strip of blue stickers, I can't help raising my eyebrows.

She smiles. "I ride my bike to work. It happens a lot." After she puts all her stickers on, she says, "It's good you're doing this. I forget I don't have to take it for granted."

Back at Vivi's, we have dinner with her family and end up

in our pajamas on her screen porch with a pan of brownies.

"This was really great," Prisha says. "Thanks for inviting me."

"It wasn't painful at all," Vivi responds. "You're way cooler than I thought."

So I guess it's time for Insult Our Friends.

"Sorry," Vivi says into the silence.

Prisha tosses her hair. "It's not like I didn't know what you thought of me. Besides, I always liked the idea of being a Cotton Candy Princess. That may be my Halloween costume this year."

Vivi's mouth opens. Mine too, and my cheeks get hot.

"Where did you hear that?" Vivi asks.

Prisha laughs. "You're a lot of things, Vivi, but subtle isn't one of them."

"Sorry..." Vivi says again.

But she's holding something back. I can tell. "Just say it."

Vivi lifts her shoulders and turns to Prisha. "I'm not trying to start a fight, but I don't understand how you can listen to all the stories we heard today and then turn around and wear makeup and short skirts and all that."

I look at Prisha, afraid she's going to get upset. But she's calm. I turn back to Vivi. "Because it matters how I was dressed that night Matt whistled at me?"

Vivi's whole face changes. "No, no. I wasn't saying that." She stops and looks off into the distance.

"Weren't you?"

"Maybe. I didn't even know I thought that. I'm so sorry. It wasn't your fault."

I lift a shoulder. "I know," and, as I say it, I realize I actually do. This afternoon, talking with girls and women of all ages, dressed all kinds of ways, in all different bodies helped move that understanding from my brain to my heart. "And yeah, I don't hate the idea of dressing up and looking pretty. But that doesn't mean I want guys to holler at me or that I don't care about my friends or that I'm going to stop answering questions in math."

"Why would you?" Prisha asks.

"And even if I start wearing makeup or skirts or whatever more often, we'll still be best friends," I say, looking at Vivi. "And we'll take coding together and sit by each other at lunch next year, and Prisha too—if she wants."

"I do!" Prisha says. She smiles a little mischievously. "I wouldn't mind sitting by Knox. He's gotten super cute all of a sudden."

I stare at Prisha, trying to figure out if she's serious.

"Careful, Prisha. Lilla doesn't like that," Vivi says. "She might take back your invitation."

"I'm sure she's just thinking about the best way to set me up with her childhood friend. Who she has no interest in," Prisha says.

"Fine," I say, giving in. "I had a little crush on Knox. But I'm over it. Or I will be. Any minute now."

"You're definitely not over it," Vivi says. "I was worried for Prisha's health and safety just now."

"My dad would have a fit if I started…" My voice trails off. Because what would I call it? I like Knox, but I don't think I'm ready to date.

"Maybe it doesn't have to be such a big deal," Vivi says. "You could hang out, the two of you sometime, let him walk you home, and maybe, if you're lucky, kiss you goodnight."

Prisha sighs, caught in the daydream. But I've been friends with Vivi a long time. There's more in her voice. She's not talking about me and Knox.

I can't keep the smile from breaking across my whole face. Like it was my first kiss. "Vivian. Did you and Colby…?"

Vivi's grin is as wide as mine. "Yesterday."

I can't believe something this big happened and she went the whole day without telling me. "Do you feel different?"

"No, I feel the same. It was fun though. You should only do it if you want to, but avoiding boys like Knox won't keep away boys like Matt. He didn't whistle at you because you were giving off some secret I-like-someone signal or because you were wearing pretty clothes. You can want to kiss Knox without it meaning anything to anyone else."

"Maybe," I say.

"Either way, you need to decide what to do. Because he's going to say something. Soon. You can say no, but be nice."

"I don't think he's about to say anything. I kind of…took care of that," I say.

"Uh-oh," Prisha says, looking at Vivi. "You're too late."

"Lilla," Vivi says, scolding me. This is where it gets complicated that Knox is her friend too.

They both stare at me in silence until I break. "We were sitting on top of the monkey bars at the museum?"

They nod, waiting for me to say more.

"And he might have reached for my hand," I whisper.

"Might have?" Vivi says.

"How can you not know?" Prisha adds.

"Well, I threw myself to the ground before it became totally clear."

CHAPTER 27

Conditions

Mom texts in the morning asking me to meet her and Dad for breakfast. The good news is leaving early ends Vivi and Prisha's teasing. They bonded last night by flinging themselves to the ground whenever I brushed up against either one of them.

My friends are very hilarious.

Mom and Dad sit facing each other at a table by the window, forcing me to choose who to sit next to. I pick Mom. I am not thrilled that she wants to move to Chicago, but at least I get where she's coming from, and she told me before she did it.

I say good morning and hide behind the menu.

"We ordered for you. Sorry," Mom says, but it doesn't seem like she means it. She pushes a glass of orange juice over.

"It's fine." I mean, I eat the same thing every single time we come here, but still, it's nice to be asked.

"We're worried about you," Dad says.

"Will," Mom breaks in.

"Kara," he echoes. "We agreed this was a problem." They're completely focused on each other. I might as well not be here.

"Just to be clear," I say into their silence, "we're here today so you can tell me *your* problems? With *me*?" I can't believe this. I wasn't looking forward to this talk, but I did think it was going to start with apologies. From them.

"Not problems," Dad says. "Concerns."

"Oh, well then."

Mom's eyebrows go up. My sarcasm is a surprise. She exchanges a look with Dad.

"This is what I'm talking about," Dad says to her. Then to me, "You haven't been yourself lately. You're moody. You dress up and come back crying. You misled us about which program you were applying to for the magnet school, and I don't think you've done any work to prepare for the showcase. For either track. Maybe it's the divorce or maybe it's that you're about to be a teenager, but either way, this isn't working."

I'm surprised when relief follows the stab of hurt his words cause. I didn't expect to be grateful they are finally seeing through all my fake smiles. But I am.

"It's been a rough couple of days, and even before, I'm not sure that—"

Mom cuts me off before I can say that bird-nesting isn't working for me. "We're sorry if we made you feel like we'd be disappointed with either magnet program."

Oh. Of course, this is what they're thinking about.

"Both the arts and STEM programs have great track records getting kids into outstanding universities. You choose whichever path seems right for you."

"Absolutely," Dad says. "I apologize if I made you feel like focusing on science wasn't an appropriate choice. You know I respect what your mother does."

He looks at Mom.

"What?" she says. "Lilla knows I respect you."

"That's not the same. When you introduced me at parties, you used to say, 'This is Will. He studies coloring in.'"

"Which you do," she says, smiling.

I can't listen anymore. Even when they're worried about me it's about themselves. How it makes them look as parents. What it says about their jobs.

"I'm not here to prove you're a good parent," I say.

They both stop.

"Or to make you feel good about yourselves or give you stories to talk about with your colleagues...or *girlfriends*."

Dad lowers his eyes. "I am sorry for not giving you a heads-up about that."

I shake it off. "I don't want to go to the magnet school. I don't know what I want to do when I grow up, but I don't want the life you have. Either of you."

"What do you mean?" Dad asks.

"I don't want to work all the time. I don't want everything to be a competition. I don't want to have to focus on one ridiculously small thing and cut everything else out of my life. I want to go to a regular school and take all kinds of classes and do color guard and art club and robotics and have friends and not worry about whether I score in the ninety-fifth or ninety-sixth percentile on some test because of what that means for my future."

"Color guard?" Dad says.

Why does everyone get caught up on that part?

Mom takes my hand. "I understand you're angry, but throwing away your future to punish us doesn't make sense."

The waitress puts down our plates. I wipe at my eyes. Without a word, she takes an extra stack of napkins out of her apron pocket and sets them by my plate. Her small kindness ruins me, and all the tears I've been holding in fall.

"We need to go back to therapy," Mom says. "You need a better handle on this divorce. It didn't happen because we worked too much."

"Is that what she thinks?" Dad asks, completely confused, and some of my anger slides away. He can't help that he doesn't get me. Or other humans.

I rub one of the napkins all over my face. "No. Or, I mean, maybe. But it doesn't matter. It's not about you. I need you to see that I am an actual real person. Not a scorecard that tells you if you're winning parenting."

Neither of them seems to want to speak after that, so I start on my pancakes, even though it's sort of a waste to eat something this bad for me when I can't enjoy it. I swirl a bite around in the caramel sauce on my plate. May as well make the most of it.

Mom takes a deep breath. She'll make the call on this. Dad follows her lead with me.

"Middle school is hard for everyone. And the divorce, and this Northwestern stuff, and your dad dating isn't making it easier. But you can't drive your life off a cliff because this summer is tough. We're your parents. It's our job to take the long view."

Dad nods. If she'd said something else, he would have gone along, but this is what he wants.

"You are going to exhibit something at the showcase and go to the magnet school. Because in a year, you will be grateful you took advantage of this opportunity, and in four years, you're going to be even happier. And if you can't bring yourself to thank us until you grow up, I can live with that."

I shake my head a little. I don't know how to make them hear me. To get them to treat me like a person, and not like their very own Magnet School Barbie.

"And because we haven't been able to trust you to get this

done," Dad continues, "you need to stay in your room today and work on your exhibit."

"And give us your phone," Mom says.

"Why?" I ask. Thinking about breaking this down with Vivi is all that's getting me through.

"We want you to focus," Dad says.

"But what's the point? I need my laptop to work. My friends have email."

Mom holds out her hand. "It's the principle. Having a phone is a privilege. You can have it back after the showcase."

"If I earn it."

"Our love is unconditional. Our technology plan is not," Mom says with a smile.

CHAPTER 28

Magnet School Barbie

Two days later, Mom raps on my door. "Ready to go?"

I take one last look in my mirror.

My pale-pink dress flares out at the waist, and my hair's coiled into a low bun with a huge silk rose clipped on the side. With pink ballet flats and lip gloss, it's a total mood.

When I come out, Mom's eyes narrow with suspicion. "What are you wearing?"

"Would you like to dress me in something else?" My voice is calm. Ever since our breakfast, I've been doing exactly as I've been told—staying in my room, working on my exhibit, coming to meals when asked, and speaking when spoken to.

But all my extra is gone.

I do not bounce into rooms or share funny little stories about my training for the science camp or laugh at anyone's jokes. I set the table when Dad asks, but do not discuss paintings. I wash the dishes for Mom, but do not sit with her when she turns the television on.

I'm not sure that Dad's even noticed the difference. Mom definitely has, but so far she hasn't said anything about it.

"We expect you to take this seriously."

"If you want me to wear something else, I'll change." Two things can happen tonight. Either my plan will work, or this is my new life, and I'll have to hide my real self behind this other, pretend Lilla. It's only five years. I can make it if I have to.

Mom presses her lips together. "No, it's fine. You look very nice." She does not like to tell me what to wear. She likes it when I figure out what she wants me to wear and put it on.

I follow her down to Dad's, grabbing my portfolio case on the way out. "Is that a clue?" he says when he sees it.

I shrug. "Everything we display has to be pinned up. It could go either way."

They haven't pressed me on whether I'm doing science or art. This is how they show what good parents they are.

Earlier, I heard Mom on the phone with someone saying, "Oh, we have no idea what she's doing. We'll find out tonight with everyone else."

They must both suspect I'm doing art because every time they've walked in on me over the last two days I've been drawing. They're not wrong.

We drive in silence to the magnet school. There's a banner out front advertising the Annual Showcase.

Gripping the handle of my portfolio, I follow my parents to the front steps.

"We'll leave you here. Parents are supposed to go around back to the cafeteria," Dad says.

I nod.

Dad hugs me. "Good luck."

"Thanks."

Mom puts her hand on my cheek and turns my face toward her. "We wouldn't be doing this if we didn't think it was best."

"I know."

And I do. And I hope when they see what I did they know the same is true about me.

A woman at the door greets me with a clipboard.

"Arts or STEM?" she asks.

"Arts."

"Visual or performing?"

"Visual."

"Studios across from the gym." Her eyes move to the boy behind me.

"Where would coding be?" I ask.

"Technology and engineering are in the library."

Figures. The school doesn't count writing as one of the arts. And I don't think people here are all that concerned about reading either. "What about the performing arts?"

"Auditorium. You're not still trying to decide, are you?" she says with a smile.

I shake my head. "Checking on friends."

"Okay, but get your own exhibit set up first. Judging starts in a half an hour."

Except for the performers, you don't get to be there when your work is judged. Which maybe is a good thing.

Everything in the school is clean and new. There's lots of stainless steel, bright-blue accents, and odd little seating pods. But no windows. Take time to enjoy nature and you might end up well rounded, I guess.

I don't see Vivi or Knox. Or Kate, who's judging tonight. So at least there's that.

I hurry down a side hall, following a couple of kids carrying portfolios like mine. The first open door leads to a clay studio with tables set up for showing off bowls and sculptures. Clara, who I know a little, is unpacking a set of vases onto one of the stands. A flash of nerves hits my stomach. What I'm doing is not exactly art. And while I don't care if I get in, I don't want to be embarrassed.

The next room is the drawing studio, and it has the only windows I've seen in the building. Reeds sway in the meadow out back, and somehow the neighborhoods around the school are completely hidden. Easels have been pushed to the center of the room up against low bookcases that hold more pens, pencils, paints, and brushes than I have ever seen all together in one place.

I do get what Mom and Dad are saying. The art classes I take at Morningside will not be in a space like this. But behind the teacher's desk are rows and rows of awards (most won by the same boy). Next to the awards is a list of some kind of rankings. There's no way I could do my best work here.

"And you are?"

I turn. A woman with a messy bun, jeans, and a silver top holds another clipboard.

"Lydia Baxter-Willoughby."

She glances at her paper. "Found you. I wasn't sure you were in the right place."

I hold up my portfolio, feeling like it makes it pretty obvious I belong here.

"I know, but the dress? I'd have guessed singer. Or maybe the flute?"

"The dress is part of the art," I say.

She grins. "Okay. Now, I'm interested. What'd you bring?"

I have to think about this. I hadn't actually thought about the art word for my project. Finally, I say, "Collage."

"Let's get you a space."

The room is designed for students to display their work. Two blank white walls are filled with tiny holes left over from thumbtacks. Most kids are hanging up either line drawings or paintings. Four to five pieces to show range. The best display is nothing but portraits done in black ink. One—an old woman—feels really sad.

The silver-top woman sees me looking at it. She nods. "It's good, isn't it?"

"Yes. It's the best in the room."

"That's generous." She's surprised. "Visual arts is one of the smallest programs. They'll only take five or six of you."

"And whoever did that should be one of them."

She laughs and points at two lines of masking tape. "Your space."

I can't believe I'm doing this.

I pin up a line drawing of myself in my floaty blue top and leggings, looking over my shoulder. Afraid. It's a bit of a rough sketch because I've only been working on it for two days, and I wanted to spend most of my time on the second drawing: two guys sitting on the front porch of their fraternity. I'm not so good that it's clearly Matt, but I think it will be close enough for Kate.

I connect the two drawings with yarn lines to a little card. In fancy lettering, it says: Come back in a few years, sweetheart.

Underneath, I put up our map, and next to that, a graph I made from Prisha's survey data.

I surround the two drawings with photographs. These are not super artsy. They were taken from my phone and printed at the drugstore. Next to each, I pin up a little caption.

Vivi: "You're not the one who needs to be embarrassed."

Matt: "Lots of girls would feel flattered."

Kate: "He shouldn't have whistled at you. But boys."

Aman: "You're a kid."

Above all of it, I place the title I got from a Twitter hashtag in careful calligraphy: The First Time I Was Catcalled.

When I step back to take it in, the woman in the silver top comes to stand by me.

"I know the drawings aren't…" I start.

"Shh," she says. "Don't apologize. It's cowardly."

So I watch her look. Her gaze catches on Kate's picture and her eyes flick to the drawing. She turns slowly toward me. "You're a junior counselor at the museum?"

I nod.

"And he works there?" She points to Matt.

I nod again.

"And Kate is Kate Krause…the education director?" This time I don't even nod. I just wait. "You know she's a judge?"

"Yes," I say.

She takes in my dress again. "Part of the art?" Her mouth quirks up at the corner.

"Kate has a lot of thoughts about how girls are supposed to dress," I say.

"Okay. First, I'm sorry this happened to you. I was thirteen the first time. Walking home from school."

This gives me an idea.

"Before you do 'second,' can I borrow some sticky notes? And a pen? Is that cheating?"

"No, I don't think so."

When she returns, I ask her to write exactly what she said on the note and put it next to my pictures. I drag a stool over and leave the notepad and the pen on top.

"Okay. Now, do second."

"You are a very quiet force of nature."

"Is that it?"

She laughs. "No. What do you want to get out of this?"

"I don't know. I don't have a wish list or anything. But I feel like she didn't take it seriously." I look back at my drawings. "And neither did he. It doesn't seem fair that I'm the only one who did."

She's quiet for a while. Then she says, "All right, my little force of nature. Let's see how this goes."

CHAPTER 29

A Complicated Jumble

I go looking for Knox and Vivi. Not being able to text them is the biggest pain ever.

The hall outside the auditorium is full of kids talking to themselves, silently playing instruments, and stretching their faces in all kinds of weird ways.

Knox sits back against the wall, curled over his guitar—the one that doesn't plug in. He's wearing jeans, a black T-shirt, and his red shoes. My hand moves toward my bag to find my sketchbook. I want to draw him like this.

He looks up before I get to him, and his mouth falls open a little. He sets his guitar aside and scrambles to his feet. "Lilla," he whispers.

Something in his voice makes me a little nervous. I don't

want him to say anything I don't want to hear. So I spin, playfully. "You like the dress?"

"I do." He holds my gaze until I look away. "Keep me company while I wait?"

"Of course." I sit, keeping plenty of space between us. "Nervous?"

"Some." He sounds like it.

"You'll do great."

He's quiet, looking down at his guitar again. "What if my voice cracks?"

"I don't know." Mostly I think growing up is harder if you're a girl. But I don't envy boys this particular thing. It's so public. "They must be used to it. Everyone's always this age when they audition. Besides, if you have a problem, you can do that growly whispery thing you do."

He looks up from his guitar. "You like that?"

"I do," I say, embarrassed because it feels like I'm admitting something new. My feelings about Knox and boys are still a complicated jumble. With everything else going on, I'm not ready to sort them out.

"How are things with your parents?" he asks.

I've sent him a couple of emails, but not as many as to Vivi.

"Not great. They're really set on me coming here."

"Would that be so terrible?" He has to know this isn't about him. Or Vivi.

"Look around. All this pressure. You can taste it. I'm

tired of feeling anxious all the time."

"You don't think it pushes you to do better?"

"That might be how it works for you, but not for me."

He nods. "Then your parents will listen. They love you."

"I don't know. They're so sure they know what's right."

"What'd you do for your exhibit? It's not a blank wall, is it? If you're not careful, you'll get admitted as some kind of modern art prodigy."

"You want to see?"

"I'm not supposed to leave. They're doing actors first, but they could start with us anytime."

"I have the rough-draft version." I pass him my sketchbook.

He grins. "Really?"

Vivi is the only one I ever let see this, but I want Knox to know, and I can't say it out loud. "The page with the ribbon."

He opens it. What I drew right after it happened. My own fear. Matt's face again and again. His words all around it.

Knox stares at the pages for a few seconds. I can't tell what he's thinking. "When?" His voice is cold.

"That night Colby found me. When I didn't come over."

"And you looked so sick at the museum the next day. I'm going to kill him." Knox's whole body tenses. Like he might leap up right now. It's sweet, so I don't point out that whatever Knox does, he's unlikely to hurt Matt.

I put my hand on his wrist. "I'm taking care of it."

Knox looks at my hand for a minute, before lifting his eyes

to mine. "This is like the door thing?"

"Yeah. If I need help, I'll let you know."

He shakes his head. "Why didn't you tell me before? I liked him."

"I didn't know what you'd do."

"Hey," he says, hurt again.

"Can you tell me you've never…"

"Of course I haven't."

"I hear boys at school," I say. "Or see them talking, even if I can't hear."

"I don't. I mean, I'm not going to say I've never talked about a girl. But nothing like this." He points at the sketchbook.

"But you've heard it."

"Yeah. Of course."

"And did you say anything to stop it?"

"No." He looks away. "Not unless it was about you or Vivi."

"Ready?" Colby bounds up to us, Vivi a few steps behind.

I get up, grateful for the excuse to stop talking about this. "What are you doing here?"

"Came with Knox," says Colby. "I'm going to throw my T-shirt at the stage when he plays."

Vivi nudges his shoulder. "Isn't it supposed to be underwear?"

Colby looks down at himself. "How would that work?"

Vivi says something I don't hear, because Knox leans into me and says, "I'll do better. Not just with you."

I squeeze his hand. "Good luck."

CHAPTER 30

Lend You My Coat

A voice over the speaker system says the monologues are over and instrumentalists should go backstage. Whoever it is also asks a few kids to report to the library for questions. Vivi gives me a panicked look.

"It's fine," I tell her. "You don't need to answer questions because your program is perfect."

Then Colby, Vivi, and I find seats in the auditorium. We sit near the front, but I stay on the aisle. I'm half expecting my parents to demand to see me at any moment.

The bottom level is only half-full, but the balcony is packed because the parents of the performers have to sit up there. Knox's mom and dad are by the railing, but on opposite sides.

I like how this school manages grown-ups—sending

them off to the cafeteria, not letting them see kids' exhibits until we're out of the way, corralling them here in the theater. When I tell Vivi this, she says, "They want to make sure our parents aren't pushing us. That we're the ones who want this."

"And yet, here I am."

She smiles. "It's not a perfect system."

The theater quiets when the lights go down. A girl from one of the other middle schools plays the flute, and she is definitely wearing a dress that looks like mine. She seems good, but not as good as Abby, a girl from our school who knew she'd never make the test score cutoff. The whole system makes no sense.

When the flute girl finishes, the audience claps politely. Except for her parents, who shout, "Brava, brava." I'm so glad I never took up an instrument.

Next come a cellist, a couple of violin players, and a trumpeter. And then a pause while a kid fusses with his drums.

"I don't really get music," Vivi says while we wait.

"What's to get?" I ask.

"The point? What are they trying to get done?"

Colby and I look at each other, trying to figure out if she's serious. I say, "You made a computer program where the goal is to defeat evil goats."

"So?" she says.

"What's the point of that?"

"To defeat evil goats," she answers.

"Obviously." Colby laughs and picks up her hand from the armrest.

When the drum solo starts, Vivi leans her head on his shoulder. I watch her out of the corner of my eye. (In part because, although I will never admit this to Vivi, I don't see the point of drum solos. Unless it's volume. In that case, mission accomplished.)

Is Vivi Colby's girlfriend now? She didn't come out and say that in our emails. But he didn't seem nervous when he reached for her hand. Vivi tilts her face up toward his and whispers something. He shakes his head, telling her to stop.

Like I would when she's pushing limits.

I get Vivi's jealousy about Prisha. It hurts to see someone else filling my role with her and knowing she wants to be with him instead of me. At least some of the time. I wonder if she was a little relieved I was grounded these last few days. So she didn't feel guilty about spending time with Colby.

We get four piano acts in a row. During the last one, a girl sings "Somewhere Over the Rainbow" while she plays. The applause afterward is much louder than for anything yet.

"I like it better when there are words," Vivi says.

I'm enough of my father's daughter to want to defend high art, but since I liked it better, too, I keep quiet.

There are two more acts before Knox comes out, carrying his guitar in one hand and a stool in the other. He sits by the mic, waiting for the judges' signal, and looks out over the audience. I wave wildly, and he grins when he sees me.

But when one of the judges raises her hand, his face gets serious, and his eyes drop to his hands. Something about the way he cradles the guitar makes my breath catch. I've never heard his song. It's quiet and sweet, but complicated enough to impress the judges. And his voice is perfect. He didn't need to worry.

Knox looks right at me when he gets to a part about wanting to lend a girl his coat. This brings an ache to my chest that I don't know what to do with. Tears pool in my eyes, even though I'm not sad—at least I don't think I am.

The applause when he finishes is even louder than for "Somewhere Over the Rainbow." Vivi and Colby holler and stand. But I don't even clap. Instead, I press my hands to my mouth, trying to hold myself together.

Vivi sits back down and wraps her arms around me. From his seat, Colby peeks around her shoulder, looking baffled. He has to be worried I'm unhinged at this point.

Someone else is playing the guitar—electric this time— and singing a much louder song, so Vivi puts her mouth right against my ear. "What is it?"

I shake my head, but she pulls back to give me a look.

I don't have the right words, but I put my mouth against her ear and whisper, "I really liked that song and the way he held his guitar and how his hair almost covers his eyes, and I think, maybe, he was singing to me. Only I don't know what to say to him and what if we never speak again and we stop being friends because it's all too weird. And I don't know how to do any of this."

She says, "You are ridiculous. A boy you like who you have been friends with forever sang you a song. This is not a tragedy." She opens her bag, digs around in it for a while, closes it again, reaches for my bag, does the same, and pulls out my sweater.

I look at her blankly.

"Wipe your face," she says. "If you'd carry tissues, you'd be a lot less hard on clothes."

I wipe my face all over my white sweater. Mascara must be for people who cry less than I do. Vivi shakes her head a little, takes it from me, and stuffs it back in my bag.

"You knew he was going to do this," I say.

"Better up your Summer Wish game. Knox won this round."

This hardly seems fair, since I'm using my showcase to go after one of the judges, but there's no point arguing with Vivi's rulings. She won't change them.

After a few more acts, a teacher comes out onstage and says there will be a break before the vocalists. He asks two kids to go to the math classroom and then says, "And if Lydia Baxter-Willoughby is here, will you please report to the studio?"

My anxiety makes me leap up. Vivi and Colby follow. When we get out into the hall, Knox is waiting, holding his guitar. His face, uncertain but hopeful, makes me forget all the panic triggered by the announcement.

"That was…wow," I say.

"Thanks." He smiles and looks at the ground. Amusement rolls off Vivi and Colby, who have been going out for forty-eight hours and are now relationship experts, apparently. Knox, thank goodness, says, "Let's put off the postgame. You should go see what they want."

"You don't have to come."

"Lilla," Vivi says, "we're coming."

Colby's confused again.

"You remember that night you walked me home?" I ask.

He nods.

"Come find out what happened."

"Oh. Okay."

Knox and Vivi text their parents while they follow me. They decide that Vivi's mom, who's here on her own, will wait and take everyone home. I'm not sure how much she knows. But probably everything.

I put my finger on my neck when we get to the art hall. My pulse is going wild. The therapist I saw after the divorce taught me some tricks for settling my body down, but none of them work right now. I have no idea what's waiting for me.

The woman in the silver top is standing outside the closed studio door.

"Hello again, Lydia," she says. "I didn't introduce myself earlier, but I'm Ms. Kornely. I teach drawing."

"I go by Lilla, actually," I say. She leans in to hear, and I force myself to speak up. "Am I in trouble?"

"No," Ms. Kornely says. Her eyes travel over my shoulder to everyone else. "But maybe your friends want to wait in the main hall?"

"I want them here. Vivi helped with the map, and Knox and Colby...I want them here."

She nods. "Okay. There are some people in there who'd like to talk to you, but you're under no obligation to speak to anyone. Except your parents. We pretty much have to send you home with them."

"No wiggle room on that at all?" I ask. "Maybe a boarding-school option?"

She laughs. "Here's the situation. You've got four judges, including me, who are split on whether you should be admitted. It's an effectiveness of message versus quality of technique debate, and we've got no tiebreaker because the one thing we all agree on is that Kate can't be impartial about this work."

"I can't believe she let him keep working there," Knox says behind me. "She's a grown-up. Isn't she supposed to know better?"

"Oh good," Ms. Kornely says. "I was afraid we might be at the end of the drama for the evening. Kate says she thought you were okay with the way she handled the situation and that your project is not appropriate. Your parents say this incident traumatized you, and you should be allowed to exhibit additional artwork. Your father keeps offering to drive home and get other pieces. Your mother is asking the assistant principal to reverse our decision."

"You've made a decision?" I say, trying to keep up.

"No, she's thinking ahead."

Sounds about right. "What do you need from me?"

"I need to know what you want."

That's easy. Go home with Vivi. Get into her mom's car and sleep at her house and pretend none of this happened. Not Matt or my parents' divorce or Kate or the magnet school or even Knox and his song. I want my old life, where I was good and quiet and everyone was happy.

But that, as Vivi would say, is not on the menu.

I look at Vivi. "I get the trophy."

"Locked up," she says.

"Open that door and it's no contest," Knox agrees.

CHAPTER 31

Summer of Brave

Every person in the room stops talking when I open the door.

Mom wraps me in her arms as soon as she can. "Why didn't you tell me?"

"You weren't here when it happened." I'm not saying this to hurt her, but it's true. If she'd been home that night, the whole story would have poured out. Since she wasn't, I turned to other people. I can't stop her from moving away, but she has to understand my life—good and bad—is going to keep going while she's gone.

She squeezes her eyes shut. "Is that what this is about? Punishing me?"

I take a deep breath. "No. This is about Matt and Kate thinking what he did was no big deal, and me deciding it was."

I turn to face the rest of the room. It's only the five judges and Mom and Dad. Dad's lips are pressed together, and his arms are crossed. From him, this is shouting. But I can't tell if he's upset at me or everyone else.

Kate's by herself in the corner. She looks teary, which doesn't feel fair. Tonight isn't supposed to be about comforting her.

A man I don't know crosses to me, "I'm Mr. Lyons, director of the arts program here."

I look over my shoulder at Ms. Kornely. "I teach at Morningside. I'm just helping with the judging." She teaches at Morningside!

Mr. Lyons says, "Is your collage an accurate representation of what happened?"

Kate starts to speak, but Ms. Kornely lifts her hand like a crossing guard, and Kate closes her mouth.

"Yes."

"You said it was a misunderstanding," Mr. Lyons says to Kate.

"He said he thought she was older," Kate says quietly.

The disgust on Ms. Kornely's face feels weirdly good. Because she's taking my side and because she agrees that Kate didn't treat this seriously enough. Mom squeezes my shoulder.

In the quiet that follows, Vivi walks over to my exhibit. Everyone watches while her eyes wander over it. I told her what I was doing, but this is the first time she's seen it.

When she's done taking it in, she reaches for the pad of sticky notes, writes something, and adds it to a dozen others now up around my work. Watching her, Colby and Knox both look sick.

"We're still making a decision, but your work obviously generates emotional response," Mr. Lyons says when Vivi returns to my side. "And your test scores are very high. I can't promise you'll be admitted, but you've got a good chance."

Dad smiles, just a little. He's relieved my work seems to be good enough. I look over my shoulder at Mom. She gives me a little nod, encouraging. Even Knox looks hopeful, as if I might have changed my mind about what I wanted from just minutes ago when we were talking in the hallway. Do I really want to make all of them unhappy? Is it worth it?

But then Vivi clears her throat, and I meet her eyes. The look she gives me is fierce, and even though she doesn't say it out loud, I hear her command: *be brave.*

"This school isn't what I want. It never was," I say. "I don't want to come here."

"No," Mom gasps.

"She doesn't know what she's saying," Dad says.

"I think Lilla is going through a difficult time," Kate says, looking between Mom and Dad. As if what I'm doing here tonight is some kind of divorced-kid-acting-out thing.

Every adult in the room looks at me. Standing in my old-fashioned pink dress, with my bun, and my flower, I open my eyes very, very wide and don't argue because I can talk back to Kate without saying a word.

Vivi's Summer Wish taught me this. Being brave isn't the same as being loud.

I turn away from Mr. Lyons and focus on Mom and Dad. "I came tonight because you made me. And I thought if I did, you might actually listen to me about school." I look over at Kate. "And I thought you might listen to me about Matt."

"Oh, Lilla," Mom says.

"This school isn't something children should be pushed into," Mr. Lyons says. "Maybe this isn't the right choice for Lilla."

"Let's just take a moment," Dad says. "She's understandably emotional. You can't hold her to this."

"Will," Mom says. She turns my shoulders so I'm facing her. "I'm sorry I wasn't listening. It must have been really scary to feel so on your own. I lost my head for a little while, but I'm back now."

I lean into her, and all the tension inside me unspools. It's going to be okay.

Dad comes over and awkwardly pats my back. Before he would have wrapped his arms around both of us. I remember what he said about my family not being destroyed, just being different, and I pull away from Mom so I can stand between them and hold both of their hands.

Dad squeezes my hand and looks at Kate.

"I don't understand what you were thinking. We work together. She's my daughter. And the kid you put in charge of her harassed her."

"I didn't want you to cause problems for the museum," Kate says. "I thought you might overreact."

"I'm going to call this," Ms. Kornely says. She's my new favorite person. "Lilla, you're sure you don't want in?"

I nod.

"Kate?" Kate looks at her. "I think you're done judging for the night. You might want to go home and think about what you want to say to Lilla tomorrow after you've had some time to consider her project. And I think you need to come up with some office work for Matt the rest of the summer. I'm not sure he needs to be supervising teen girls."

"I love that woman," Vivi says loudly. "I'm going to learn to draw and go to school with Lilla." Colby puts his hand over her mouth.

Kate looks at Ms. Kornely and Mr. Lyons and Dad. On her way out, she stops in front of me. "I was twelve the first time," she says. "On the bus. My mom said it was because my skirt was too short. I'm sorry I didn't take you seriously."

I almost say it's okay. But it's not, so instead, I say, "Thank you."

CHAPTER 32

Hold Your Hand

After getting a teary goodbye and a promise not to stay out too late, Mom lets me leave with everyone else. Vivi's mom drops us off downtown for ice cream, but after we get our cones, we end up on the sidewalk, looking at each other in awkward silence.

On the way back in the car—much to the delight of Vivi's mother—we'd rehashed everything that happened in the art room, so now we've said everything there is to say.

Almost everything.

Colby takes Vivi's hand. "Want me to walk you home?"

"Yes, please, but let's go the long way."

Colby exchanges some kind of look with Knox and then says to me, "Good night, troublemaker."

Vivi pouts. "I thought that was me."

He shakes his head. "Lilla took the title tonight."

The silence when Knox and I are alone hits all new levels of awkward. It expands with every second. Like some kind of awkwardness fractal. It's a huge relief when he says, "River rock?" Both because it's something to do and something familiar.

Mostly to have something to say, I tell him, "I can't stay out too late. My parents want to talk to me."

"I can imagine. I need to get back too. I'm headed to my dad's for a couple days."

"How's that going?"

"Okay, I guess. My mom talked to him, and he's trying harder. He was there tonight."

"I saw him." And my cheeks heat because I'm thinking about Knox onstage again. "When's he picking you up?" I ask before the silence gets too long again.

"I'll text him. He can get me at your house after I walk you back."

This is one of those things we do but never talk about—Knox's habit of walking me home after twilight.

"I wish I felt comfortable walking back on my own."

He smiles. "I like walking you home."

I sort through the tangle of feelings caused by that sentence—and lately, by Knox. I'm glad he likes being with me, and if I'm honest, I like that he wants to look out for me. But I'm angry about it too. That it's necessary.

Knox reads the confusion on my face. He skims his hand over his head. "That was me and your point, huh? You just want to be able to walk home on your own. Like I do."

"Yeah. All those things that make you feel strong—opening doors and walking me home and growling about Matt—make me feel weak."

He huffs, making his hair fly up in the air, which is real cute, so I add, "But also protected."

"Girls are confusing."

"Only when we're confused."

We're quiet then, and we watch the stone he's kicking along the sidewalk. When we get to the little path that leads to our rock ledge, he reaches in front of me to lift branches out of the way. Then he freezes, panicked.

I grin. "Thank you."

Making a big show of it, he wipes his forehead.

Even though the sun's setting, the rock's still warm. I lay back, deciding not worry about whether my pink dress gets dirty. My eyes are closed, but I feel Knox lie down, a little ways away.

"It's confusing now," I say, going back to what we were talking about. "But it might be better in the long run than it was for our parents."

"Maybe. Mom says she didn't even know who she was when they got married. Much less who she wanted to be with my dad."

"And it seems like there are more and more ways you can be—on your own or with someone else. I like that."

Knox doesn't answer except to stretch out his arms so our fingers barely touch. I don't know if this is on purpose or by accident. Then he scoots a little closer, and his fingers slide over mine. On purpose then.

Even though his hands are warm, his touch makes me shiver, and I pull back. But Knox's hand closes around mine, not letting me go. I turn my head to look at him.

He smiles. "Is it so bad? Holding my hand?"

"No," I whisper. It isn't bad at all. It's nice. I like the way he folds my fingers inside of his because it makes me feel taken care of. But liking that scares me.

Because I'm only just learning to take care of myself. I take my hand back and sit up.

Knox does too. We cross our legs, facing each other, inches between our knees, but it's not comfortable. He's disappointed, which makes me feel guilty.

"Do you not like me at all?" he asks, eyes on the ground.

"You know I like you."

He gives me a not-having-it look.

"Why me?" I ask.

"Is that what this is about? I did this wrong? I should tell you how great you are first?"

"No," I say, embarrassed. "This isn't a test. But why not Vivi?" Until right now, I didn't know I was worried about this, but I need to know that Knox didn't pick me because I was a nearby girl-shaped person. I want him to have a reason other than Colby already liked Vivi.

"Truth?" he says with a wry smile.

"Naturally."

"I'm not sure. I could list a hundred things I like about you. But I could do that for Vivi too. But when I look at her, my heart doesn't speed up. Maybe it's because you know what divorce is like. Or because you get me when I talk about music. And you say things I go to bed thinking about. And you have this smile that says you're thinking something but not saying it. Only sometimes I know what you're thinking anyway. And that's the best."

It's hard not to be swept away by this, but I want to be careful. "I don't want things to change between us. I still want to play with blocks and argue about doors and hang out with Vivi without it being weird. And when I have an idea, I want you to listen to me. And treat me like I'm a whole person."

He pulls back a little. "You think I don't want those things?"

"I think if you're thinking about me *like that*, you might want something else."

"Lydia Edith Baxter-Willoughby," he says slowly. There's a depth to his voice that's unfamiliar, but a little fascinating. I meet his eyes. "Just because sometimes I think about you *like that* doesn't mean it's the only way I think about you. I still want to work at the museum and look at your sketches and mock you for your hopeless paintball skills. I just want to hold your hand sometimes while I'm doing it."

"That's all?"

"For now," he says with a smile that makes everything inside me flutter.

"Okay," I say.

He stands and holds his hand out. And even though I could get up by myself, I let him pull me up. When we turn to walk back to my house, he doesn't let go. And I don't pull away.

CHAPTER 33

New Room

At home, I try Dad's first. No one's there, but a note on the table tells me to go up to the attic.

Maybe he's setting up a studio? We always planned to do one up there, but we haven't had time. If I'm not going to the magnet school, he probably wants me to spend more time on art at home, which is fine. I don't want to stop drawing. I just want to do other things too.

Halfway up the third flight of stairs, I hear Mom say, "This is all you. Two hundred pounds of notebooks from high school."

Dad laughs. "Tape that back up. There are drawings in there you don't want to see."

"It's not me you have to worry about."

They are so weird. I understand why Knox's parents got

divorced. His dad fell for the babysitter, and now they can't stand to be in the same room. But Mom and Dad seem happier now than they've ever been. I guess that's the answer. They're better living apart.

Mom's laughter settles me a little. Despite her words at the showcase, I was afraid of what I might come home to. We don't do shouting, but Mom and Dad are both pretty good at letting me know when they're not happy.

"What are you doing?" I ask from the door.

The attic is two big rooms with ceilings that rise to a peak in the center. Windows in the front and back let in lots of light—which is why it will make such a great studio. But right now, the only things inside are boxes from the move that never got unpacked.

"We're cleaning your room," Dad says.

This makes no sense. That girl in *The Little Princess* had to go live in the attic when her dad died, but even if Mom and Dad are more unhappy than I thought, this seems a little extreme.

"I don't…"

Mom sits down on a cardboard box and pats the space next to her. Dad sinks to the floor and leans back against another giant box.

When I sit, Mom says, "We've been thinking about all the things you've said. Tonight. This year. And all the things you haven't said. We don't want you to feel like you have to hide from us."

I still don't know what this has to do with the attic, so I wait.

"We've been telling ourselves that as long as we did the divorce right, it didn't have to affect you."

"But it did," Dad says.

Obviously, I want to say. But now that they're finally getting it, that feels like rubbing it in.

"We weren't making each other happy," Mom says. "And it was getting worse and worse. We can't stay together. Even for you."

"I know," I say quickly. This was a major theme from our year in therapy.

"But we can do a better job listening," Dad says. "You don't like moving back and forth all the time. And you're right. It's hard not to have something that feels like yours. So..." He motions to the attic.

My. New. Room.

The same bed to sleep in every night. Bookshelves and sketchbooks and a desk and my computer all in one place.

"Really?" I say.

"Really," Mom says. "We're going to put an alarm on the back door for safety, so we'll have to get used to that, and for now, you'll have to go downstairs for the bathroom, but in a year or two, we might be able to put something up here."

"Can we bring up a bed for Vivi?"

Mom laughs. "Sure."

"Can she come over tonight?"

"It's late. Let's save the sleepover for tomorrow," she says. "But we can bring a mattress up for you tonight if you want."

"But not quite yet," Dad says. "We need to talk about a couple other things."

"Okay," I say. Nervousness washes over me again.

"I'm sorry about the dating thing. You were right. When I started seeing people, I should have told you."

I nod once.

"But I don't plan to be serious about anyone for a while. And I'd rather not have people coming in and out of your life."

"Okay." It's not like I actually want to talk about stuff like this. I just want to know what's going on. I think of something else. "Are things going to be weird at the museum with you and me and Kate?"

"Probably. Yeah. There's a lot of people not happy with how she handled this. Mr. Lyons is on the board, so there are going to be some conversations. But you don't need to worry about it."

"What about you?" I say to Mom.

"I'm not happy with Kate either," she says.

I smile. "No. I mean…are you dating?" It's unfair, but her dating scares me so much more.

She shakes her head. "Not yet. I'm sure I will. But right now I'm focused on work. And you. I won't go if you tell me you can't handle it, but I do want to try Northwestern. And I don't want to ask you to move. I hope someday you'll see me going after what I want as a good thing. Even for you."

Mom has tears in her eyes, which wrecks me. I never wanted her to have to choose between me and her work. "I understand," I say. "Really. I'm so proud of you."

Yes, in my perfect world, my mom would be in my house with me every day. But I know she loves me wherever she is. And I don't want her to give up her dreams for me.

Even if her dreams are about bugs.

"And we're going to text every day. If something horrible happens to you or something really good, I want to hear about it from you. Not read about it in an art installation."

I feel guilty and proud at the same time. I made an art installation.

"Same," Dad says. "I know it's harder to talk to me about some of this. But I want us to find a way. Maybe you can show me your sketches as a way in."

This seems like a good idea, but the truth is when I open my sketchbook, Dad barely takes a breath before jumping in about my composition or line fluidity or whatever.

"Maybe," I say. "If you can promise to talk to me about what I'm drawing—and not just criticize my technique."

"I don't—" He stops. "I kind of do, don't I?"

I nod.

"I'll work on that."

"I'm sorry I hid everything from you," I say. "I'm going to work on that."

"You did great, kiddo, but you shouldn't have had to do it alone. We're going to try more listening. I think you may be wrong about the magnet program, but you shouldn't do it only because we push you into it."

"And whatever you do with your life, we'll be proud. And we'll love you. But you need to tell us what's going on," Mom says. "Deal?"

"Deal," I answer.

"Let's get your mattress then," Dad says.

On the way down the stairs, I remember I'm still hiding something, so I say, "One more thing?"

Mom turns back from her door, and Dad looks up from the stairs below me.

"Knox might be my almost-boyfriend."

CHAPTER 34

Enough

"And then what did they say?" Vivi asks the next night. We're sitting cross-legged on one of my twin mattresses.

"My dad said I was too young to have a boyfriend, even an almost one, and Mom said 'Will, we talked about this,' and he said, 'Oh, no we did not,' and 'What does she mean *almost-boyfriend*? Is that some sort of code?'"

Vivi puts her hands over her mouth and giggles, but I don't stop.

"And Mom said, 'It's kind of like those women you're seeing are *almost* your girlfriend,' and he got real quiet. And then Mom said Knox is a sweet boy, and I would be lucky to have him as my first boyfriend and Dad said, 'First!'—which honestly is the same thing I was think-ing—and then he went into his house. And Mom told me he needed to get used the idea, and in a few weeks, I'd be thirteen, and it wouldn't freak him out so much."

"Wow," Vivi says.

"I know. It was bananas. He almost pulled his hair out, and he kept pacing up and down the steps. I was worried he was going to somersault to the bottom and we'd have to call 911."

"You were okay though?"

"Yeah." It helped that I knew he wasn't really, truly angry. But I'm also getting better at calming myself down. I kept telling myself it was going to be over and he still loved me and he wasn't going anywhere, and that kept me from saying things I didn't believe to make it stop.

"Well, I'm glad you and Knox worked everything out," Vivi says.

"I don't know about *everything*. But we're definitely... in talks." I look closely at her. "You're really not bothered? Not about us—" I flap my hands around wildly.

Vivi laughs. "We're going to have to come up with words you can say out loud. But no, I'm not worried. I'm not letting go of either one of you."

"Thank goodness for that," I say. "Without you, Vivi, I'd be so much less than I am."

"Without you, I'd be a lot more judgy. You see nice things in everyone."

"Not everyone," I say, thinking of Matt.

"No," she agrees. "But what came out of it was good. There were a lot of college parents there last night. People want to do something about that map of yours."

"Ours," I correct.

"Ours," Vivi echoes. "Which reminds me, I have something for you." She pulls out what looks like a baseball wrapped in pink tissue paper.

"What is it?"

"A housewarming present."

"I have a house!" I say. I don't have air-conditioning or a bathroom or even a whole bed yet, but I have this space. And it's mine.

Slowly, I unwrap Vivi's present. It's a baby food jar. With a perfect white fluffy dandelion curled inside.

"Why?"

"Because you're brave enough to make a real wish now."

"Do I get to tell you and Knox what to do?"

"Nope. This one's just for you."

I turn the jar around in my hand. "Should I do it now?"

Vivi nods.

We go to the front window and fuss with the screen. When we get it out, I see how high up we are. "My parents are going to be real mad if I fall to my death my second night up here."

"Don't lean out. Just blow."

Taking the dandelion out the jar, I look up at the sliver

of moon. It's hard to imagine a wish that feels big enough for tonight. Especially because I already have the things that I want. A home that feels like mine. Parents who are trying to listen. Friends who won't leave because I don't want the same things. The strength to be my quiet, complicated, ordinary self.

So maybe that's my wish?

I hold the dandelion to my lips and blow as hard as I can. The little white parachutes float off into the dark, and I wish that I always remember this thing I know tonight.

I am enough.

Acknowledgments

A big thank you to my agent, Elizabeth Bennett, always, but especially for this one. I wrote it only because you said I could write a middle grade book with such conviction that I had no choice but to believe you.

Also, so many thanks my editor, Jonathan Westmark, who believed in my story about a quiet, introverted girl. I'm so thankful for all the work you did helping me get Lilla to sound exactly like herself. Truly, I am so appreciative of the whole Albert Whitman team. Designer Valerie Hernández and illustrator Jensen Perehudoff gave me the cover of my dreams before I even knew to dream it. Thank you also to Lisa White and everyone else who has worked to get *Summer of Brave* out into the world.

I am, as always, ever grateful for One Direction. My

writing playlist would be quite short without them. Obviously, "I Want to Write You a Song" is what Knox plays for Lilla at the audition.

I should also thank the gifted education scholar whose advice (written on a poster I walked by every day for seven years) telling children not to waste their energy being well-rounded made me so thoroughly irritated I had to write a book about it.

Mom and Dad, I will never be able to thank you enough for the outrageous confidence you've always had in me, even when I was quite small. Thank you for letting me make the University of Wisconsin-Milwaukee my playground, so I could give that life to Lilla, Vivi, and Knox. The lemonade stand and the sled mowing down undergraduates are both real memories of mine. (I left out how I used to slide down that metal ramp in middle of the escalators in the union because they all have those little speed bumps now, so no one would believe it.)

Thanks to Chloe and Sophie for being early readers on this, for sharing your childhoods with me, and for not letting the outrageous achievement culture that surrounds university families get to you.

Perry. Thank you for everything, big and small, from lending me Cookie Mistake to being a safe harbor during this absolutely bonkers year.

Katie Murray

AMY NOELLE PARKS is a former elementary school teacher who now helps prepare future teachers at Michigan State University. When she's not using One Direction lyrics as writing prompts (which is often), she's helping future teachers recover from the trauma inflicted on them by years of school mathematics. Amy lives in Michigan with her husband and two daughters. She is also the author of the YA romantic comedy *The Quantum Weirdness of the Almost-Kiss*.